Ragnarok,

A Plausible Future

"The world as we 'know' it will end, but we'll get to know

the world as it really is a lot better."

Jan Lundberg, Culture Change Letter #100

Brian —
I hope this effort sparks
some interesting conversations...
Best,
Jana

Ragnarok, A Plausible Future

Tuna Cole

www.ragnarokaplausiblefuture.com

Cover art by Pip Cole
Back cover photo by Doug Tracy

Ragnarok, A Plausible Future
Tuna Cole
Copyright 2009
ISBN: 978-0-578-03190-3

www.ragnarokaplausiblefuture.com

First printing: August 2009

Foreword

For the uninitiated, the title *Ragnarok* comes from Old Norse. I've anglicized the spelling by omitting the umlaut over the final vowel; few readers are Norse scholars who could benefit from the distinction. In Norse mythology, Ragnarok is a saga of the war of the gods, in which most of the participants kill each other, culminating in the near-total destruction of the earth. Among the gods and giants who perished in that heroic battle were Thor, Odin, Freya, and Loki. There *was* a rebirth, however; a few gods and humans managed to survive, thereby accounting for our presence. This ancient tale parallels many of humankind's traditional tales of 1) struggle and travail, yet eventual rise to greatness, 2) downfall and destruction resulting from unrestrained hubris, and 3) at least the potential for redemption/rebirth. It is an apt metaphor for my story.

The *plausible future* of the subtitle envisions a very different future than a projection/expansion of our current social structure. It is this *other* vision that drives the writer's conceit: that a societal Collapse is beyond preventing, and the Collapse will be so severe that many people will die—of hunger, disease, or as a result of the desperate contest for the remaining food stocks. Thus, the Fall of the Gods: the rapid disintegration of all that is familiar and most of what we hold dear. *How* this Collapse is to occur, what will precipitate it, is not known and perhaps unknowable in advance—there are simply too many strong contenders for the initiating event! We are not engineering our way out of this worsening predicament; we lacked not the technology, but the will when it might have made a difference.

This assertion will strike many as the raving of a lunatic. However, if I'm not giving away too much, a central theme of the story explores what it means to be crazy in a society that is itself, in too many ways, paranoid, sociopathic, stone-cold wacko. It remains my continued attempt to draw attention to the looming Cataclysm, and to give an indication, to point a way, wherein some people might salvage the basis for a renewed vision of community.

Those who take steps to anticipate this Collapse may not find the transition utterly devastating. In my estimation, the single most important requisite in surviving beyond the second year post-Collapse will be the ability to grow enough cereal carbohydrates, or their equivalents, to carry on between harvests. Those people who succumb to the Siren's song—the dominant narrative—to accept things as they are *(Don't worry, be happy! The more you spend the more you save!)*; those who ignore the signs and fail to anticipate this dire outcome face, and some would say, deserve the fate of the herd, always reacting to the threat after its arrival. To survive at all, such people face a brutal and bestial existence.

Mine is a story of how some people with few practical skills discover meaningful, productive interdependence as they build community and avoid a pointless and premature death. Hopefully, I offer something more than a bestial existence.

Contents

PART I

It's the same story the crow told me,
it's the only one he knows
Like the morning sun he comes
and like the wind he goes
Ain't no time to hate,
barely time to wait...
Wha-ho, what I want to know,
how does this song go?

Uncle John's Band,
The Grateful Dead

A young man raises his head very slowly into the open air of the subway station entrance and scans full circle for human activity. The skyline to the east is starting to "pink up," as a post-operative surgeon might say. There is no movement, no sound, but he is in no hurry so he pauses to identify landmarks for future orientation. The stark edges of buildings, power poles, and a few urban-showcase trees are becoming distinct. No other lighting is visible because electricity is no longer available.

The local grid started failing in mid-May and by June lighting, refrigeration, heating and cooking, assuming anyone left in the city had anything left to cook, were things of the past. Truth to tell, electrical power, thanks to large-scale hydro and wind systems on the regional grid, outlasted most of the people. Ultimately, without food the urban residents had to take a chance and leave the barren city for an unwelcoming countryside.

One year previously, Hoben Crow had been among the throng streaming out of this entrance, in his case chasing down a job and appearing for an interview. Within days of that unproductive event, a growing petroleum scarcity reached crisis level; gasoline had crashed the $12/gallon ceiling and was here and there not available at any price. In April, the administration had, without fanfare, authorized the Strategic Petroleum Reserve to release fuel, extending the long-distance trucking of food stocks and essential medicines. This maneuver was good for about six weeks until warehoused food and other stored supplies were depleted, at which time the president decided to hoard the remainder of this critical fuel and turned off the SPR spigot.

In one of those coincidences historians might in a future time delight in pouring over, China then decided publicly to call in her chips, to announce a divestiture of her US Treasury Bonds and other securities. As the country's largest foreign debt holder, China's move was the final straw; within 48 hours Japan and other global stakeholders followed suit, and it was instantly apparent that we were unable to pay off this foreign debt; Merka was bankrupt. The Fed had tried to take the edge off the looming financial crisis by "increasing liquidity," or "making more money available"—literally printing more of it. This had the inevitable effect of further devaluing the already shrunken greenback against virtually all foreign currencies. Hyperinflation was no longer deniable.

Crow hadn't been back to this site in the ensuing year and would not've imagined he might return on foot. At the moment he was intent on avoiding contact with other survivors. Previous foragers had learned the hard way that solitary or paired travelers in contested lands were prey to the last remaining marauder holdouts; all bets were off in an encounter with these sweeties. They tended to be well-armed and would take advantage of you any way they could, including killing you outright. Desperate people have always committed desperate acts if they believed it might buy them another day, another mile, though this savage truth was rarely a part of anyone's personal experience in the life Before. In those days, it was convenient to ignore such a possibility, especially since mainstream media of every stripe failed to alert the populous of the worsening threat.

If Crow had been alone as opposed to solitary—the last surviving member of a group, say, or having been banished from a tribe—he would have had to roll the dice and seek out another alliance to enhance his chances of survival. Which is exactly what he'd done early on; he'd fallen in with a loose affiliation of folks who'd been fortunate enough to have endured the early phase of the Great Collapse, lucky enough to have found a place suitable for post-Apocalypse survival before the unraveling. The tribe he was permitted to join comprised less than twenty people, with tentative contacts with other tribes in the watersheds of the surrounding area; such people hung onto the prospect of growing and raising enough food to sustain themselves.

Meanwhile, before fully relearning what their ancestors a century ago took for granted, survivors had to scavenge from the vacant remnants of the previous, unsustainable incarnation of humanity. Simply, it was Crow's turn to forage an area of the abandoned metropolis for tools, equipment, or materials he could carry back to his ragtag tribe some 30 miles up the valley and into the foothills from the city. Virtually every building in the city had been ransacked at least once for any kind of food, be it canned or packaged in dried form, by people in search of anything edible. In the throes of the Collapse everything was fair game, anything was possible.

Within six weeks of the previous April, you couldn't buy a loaf of bread, no matter how many bushels of money you had. Within two months, the US government had given up the charade that it had somesort of plan to lead the nation out of this economic and political calamity. By late-July you were, in order of statistical probability, either 1) dead, 2) hunkered down with a small group of people, having pledged a willingness to share resources and fealty to each other in the face of external threats, or 3) you'd sidled toward the camp harboring those few remaining predators. There just wasn't any other niche of livelihoods.

Crow would normally have had an accomplice on this venture. Foraging contested lands was always risky, and going in pairs was the norm. But by last evening at the recently-established safe house, the agreed upon meet-up site, when Paco failed to show, Crow opted to go ahead without him. He'd ridden from the homestead most of the way on one of the tribe's scavenged bicycles, stashing it safely at the safe house; from there on, he hoofed it. He carried in a large backpack a pocketknife, a two D-cell flashlight with fairly new batteries, a light raincoat in case he encountered a shower, and a resealable plastic container of berry-flavored oat gruel, his sustenance for the duration of his foray. Also, he had a .38 semi-automatic with an extra clip in an easy-to-reach pocket of his pack.

His attire came from thrift stores in pre-Collapse days: worn jeans; non-descript dark tennis shoes; a long-sleeved, checked, cotton shirt over a dark T-shirt; a jacket of intermediate protection against severe cold (not likely to be encountered at the outset of spring) or hard rain (never to be ruled out in the Pacific Northwest); and a floppy beige canvas hat. Also, he wore a wind-up watch; there was no presumption of any sort of accuracy calibrated to anything, let alone Greenwich Mean Time, but it was useful in measuring intervals: What time did he start/how long had he been walking? When had he eaten last? Roughly, how many more hours of daylight remained?

With a waning moon, occluded by the occasional passing array of clouds, he had enough light to make out most of his way toward the city along a highway. From the end of the subway line, he walked the last two stations underground, during which a flashlight had been a necessary if occasional aid. Other tribal members and, in rotation, he, too, had canvassed other areas of the city, honing discovery skills in the searches. Foragers were always to bring back the most valuable finds they could manage. Precious items too bulky, heavy, or numerous to carry back were to be cached or otherwise hidden from other foragers. Anything else of remote value was to be inventoried. Neighborhood by section of the city, their systematic search had yielded most of their stock of tools and hardware, weapons, virtually all their cooking/eating ware, clothes, and books (they had some small-scale agriculture and animal husbandry literature "on extended loan" from the county library).

Scavenging the old order was early understood to be the key to their initial success. Their intent was to acquire as many of the critical items as they could before the competition got more heated from pockets of other survivors. At such time, hopefully already well-provisioned, they thought to back off from the free-for-all for the remaining low-value pieces and scraps.

He had committed to memory a list of high-priority items sought by the tribal council: From any pharmacy or the bathroom medicine cabinet of any home, pain-killers (Vicodin, Percocet, Darvon, Oxycodone, morphine, aspirin), sealed syringes, sterilized gauze/bandages, and disinfectants. Retail outlets as well as homes were still reliable sources of soap and detergent; rolls of tape as well as other binding material: twine, rope, wire, and manageable lengths of small-gauge cable; fasteners of all types: the gamut of nails, bolts, and screws; unused batteries; and while a long shot at this late date, a close inspection of every kitchen/storehouse/pantry cupboard sometimes yielded overlooked flour, sugar, corn meal, dried whole grains, and legumes. Then, of course, clothes and footwear of virtually any style or size was always in demand.

This was virgin turf as far as his tribe was concerned; as long as he logged his course and noted his finds, it didn't matter where he started. He vaguely remembered a hardware store about a block away to the west. Perfect. With shadows at his back, he would be somewhat less visible to a sentinel west of the station, should there be one, than if their positions were reversed. Picking a course where the path was visible and in shadows where possible, he set out. Go directly to the hardware store and work his way back, or canvass the buildings along the way? He opted to take the buildings as he came to them. There were rarely any more locked doors since the month of the Collapse when a secured door was prima facia evidence of hoarding and was promptly pried, jimmied, or bashed open.

The 7-11 on the corner had enough parking for 8~10 vehicles on the asphalt in front. Now, only one vehicle, a late-model Buick, sat moldering back into the surface, tires flat, windshield shattered. Debris littered the remaining lot. Vandals had thrown rocks through the plate-glass windows along the front, and whole sections were completely open to the elements. Making a crunching sound on the glass under foot, Crow stepped through the shattered sliding glass door and paused to get used to the dimmer interior. He didn't expect to find anything of value in the single-story building owing to the likelihood of having been thoroughly picked over several times previously. Still, it was understood they were to physically inspect every structure they encountered: A large room with rows of empty shelving. Some damage/destruction; broken/smashed items along with more broken glass on the floor.

He walked gingerly through the room, consciously giving the front room a cursory review. With the exception of a handful of ball-point pens, which he stripped from their plastic-and-cardboard wrappings and put in his bag, virtually everything remotely useful had been appropriated. In the bathroom and cubbyhole office, he needed the flashlight but not for long; what remained—a utility desk and chair, a file cabinet in the office, a toilet, sink, paper dispenser—was pretty much intact. A quick look out the back: a 150-gallon propane cylinder (gauge read empty), and a dumptser padlocked to a steel pole anchored in cement. *Hmmm. A 6'x4'x4' lockable steel box on wheels may have some utility in the future, no matter what it might smell like now. Better make a note of it, as well as the steel racks used in the standing refrigerated cases... duly accounted.* In and out in maybe 5 minutes; a quickie!

The second structure on the right was a beauty salon on the first floor, probably apartments on the 2nd floor. Entering this hair-beautification emporium, Crow scanned the entry room: a series of padded chairs with tables between for cups/glasses, ashtrays and accessories, now nothing except tattered remnants of *haute couture*, in willful, oblivious denial, teetering on the brink of *Ragnarok* —the complete meltdown and unraveling of the fabric of the social order—as depicted in the likes of *Vogue, Maxim,* and *Harper's Bazaar.* Against the back wall were mirrors and cabinetry and five specialty sinks fronted by five lower-backed "dentist chairs" that allowed you to recline nearly horizontally while an attendant gave you a luxurious shampoo. Another attendant would be on hand to perform a manicure, if the customer felt like being really indulgent. On one side, a quartet of stainless-bonneted-chair units. For rendering a permanent? Crow had no idea. He was having a hard time conjuring how these apparatuses were intended to work, let alone to what possible use they might be put currently, and drawing a blank. *From this vantage point, sheer decadence*, was his simple conclusion. At the back of an upper shelf in the stockroom, he found a tube of some chemical compound intended to be mixed in small amounts with other toxic compounds in the service of curling one's hair —or was it straightening it? Fairly caustic shit, he was pretty sure but without knowing one way or the other, Crow tucked the unopened tube in his pack; if he came on obviously more valuable booty, he could always chuck it out—or better yet, stash it—at that location.

Out the back to locate the stairway to the second floor. Two studio apartments. At the head of the stairs, Crow entered the first unit. A twin-bed mattress on box springs, *sans* sheets or blankets, a small table, a couple of chairs, a table lamp, and chest of drawers, two of the drawers on the floor, receipts, letters, clippings scattered everywhere. The furniture was too bulky and out of place at the present level of existence; *Let's hope we'll again live comfortably enough to justify overstuffed chairs,* Crow thought. He was able to glean nearly three sets of cheap, stainless flatware from the sink and from a cupboard drawer, still food-encrusted. Crow wrapped them in a dishtowel and added them to his pack. A couple of sets of high heeled shoes sat on the floor of the meager closet: *Useless!* Some cocktail dresses of synthetic fiber were on the closet floor too: Not a chance. A little more rummaging around without reward and Crow was out the door skirting the outside walkway to the second apartment. In which, on opening the unlocked door, he encountered the apartment's occupant...

* * * * *

Throughout history up to the prior century, communities working together without the benefit of petroleum or natural gas were the norm; cooperating was the only way they could have prevailed. People in those days, of necessity, kept far more work animals (at less than a third of the human population, *millions* more horses than in current times!) to perform as much of the brute work as they could manage. In the planting season around 1910, on the cusp of the petroleum boom, future-president Harry Truman plowed and planted 70 acres in oats in one week, with the considerable aid of four horses.

The vast majority of Americans in the first decade of the 21st century, in the lead up to the Collapse, did not have the faintest inkling of what it takes to raise and train horses or oxen to pull a plow. Nor did the average American know how many fertile, plowed acres it would take to grow what kind of grain to produce enough carbohydrates/ calories to keep x number of people alive for a year—critical knowledge with a very steep learning curve. Much too short a time for most folks, it soon became apparent.

* * * * *

Holy shit, what's that? Crow said, startled, and in the instant of saying, knew it was a body, in bed and mostly covered, extending a nap throughout eternity. He took a couple of minutes to examine the clothing (a nightgown), along with the contents and décor of the room, to determine gender. The closet held a modest woman's clothing: subdued colors and patterns, nothing too exotic or revealing here. Accoutrements of a woman's toilette occupied surfaces and a drawer in the bathroom.

The woman had apparently died late last spring during or not long after the Collapse; Crow was consciously grateful for the timing. Judging from the blankets on the bed and the clothes laid out, the weather had still been cool and rainy. She had decayed primarily throughout last

13

summer, now nine or ten months ago. What remained was sallow, desiccated skin drawn taut over the skull, lips pulled back from a slightly opened mouth, two rows of yellowed teeth guarding the entrance in rictic grin. Sunken eye sockets, a little hair, sinew, and the clear outline of cranial bones. Undisturbed all these months, there was no longer any pronounced stench of decaying flesh, just a faintly musty, fetid, stale presence he found commonplace in rooms closed up for a long time. The bedding was soiled with long-dried body fluids; along with a patina of dust. The room was strewn with dead insects and their casings.

What had she died from, starvation? Or did she choose some pharmaceutical means? There was no sign of violence. As expected, the cupboards were stripped of anything edible, as was the small refrigerator, long deprived of electricity. Still, the place was eerily tidy. Far from being sacked, it had been gone over quickly and carefully, if at all. Judging from the plaster cross on the wall and Bible on the nightstand, she must have been a devout Christian. The review of her outfits hanging in the closet and in a small chest of drawers—practical, functional city shoes on the floor, no high heels in the lot—suggested a modest, middle-aged, single woman, perhaps working at a clerical job in the area. Crow imagined this woman lying low and scrimping days, even weeks, under worsening conditions, her meager food stores shrinking piecemeal, finally exhausted, believing up to the end that virtue was (or certainly should be) rewarded; that her God and her nation would rescue her. Should they fail her, well, she'd lived a virtuous life. She was ready for her reward in the Hereafter, secure in her worthiness, as demonstrated by her devotions.

He had a cursory look through the desk drawer, deliberately avoiding learning specifics about this woman; no names, please. Anonymity minimized the burden in these circumstances. *Eleanor Rigby will do,* he thought to himself. Toward the back of the stockings/underwear drawer, he found a small jewelry case, in which was housed a set of perhaps-pearl earrings, along with a couple of rings set with semi-precious stones, and a silver necklace. He left the lot; such tokens of adornment he considered affectations and vanities from a decadent past and, as such, reviled. *Let someone else pack this shit outta here, if they value it,* Crow thought.

What was surprising was not that he'd come across a dead person—over the last several months, he had discovered some half dozen—but that he'd encountered so few. In a metropolitan area of upwards of a million people just a year ago, where had they all gone? Without petroleum (or natural gas) to bring them food, and other vital necessities, without gasoline to take them where there

15

might be such resources, where could they go? No one could say for sure; however, it was clear that such a population could not have gotten far on foot (*or bicycles?*), and most had died literally unfortunate and unpleasant deaths.

Increasingly emboldened, out in the open, natural scavengers must've had a field day, he thought. What coyotes and feral dogs there were in the vicinity of exurbia during the Crash had to've experienced a brief but phenomenal surfeit of carrion. To be shared by what? Some bear, likely. More likely, rodents, skunks, and other nocturnal denizens, to say nothing of the Phylum Arthropoda—*a la* Eleanor Rigby, back there in the apartment over the Beauty Salon. Cannibalism? When push had definitely come to shove, did some very hungry people dine on their less-fortunate brethren, like something out of a Cormac McCarthy novel? He'd heard stories. It didn't pay to dwell on it...

Many people on the outskirts of the city, who'd eked out somesort of livelihood from the land—a filbert orchardist, say, or a truck farmer supplying produce to the local farmer's market—were, initially at least, better situated and provisioned to withstand the early phases of the Collapse. Left on their own, many of these people straddling two worlds, rural as well as urban, might have survived to form agrarian partnerships and alliances, and reestablish mutually supportive communities. In most cases, however, such people were overrun in a matter of weeks by the desperate hordes streaming out of the city. Desperate people do desperate things...

Crow gathered together a few towels and sheets from a small pantry near the bathroom, a couple of bars of soap, bottles of aspirin and rubbing alcohol from the medicine cabinet, the shoes from the closet, and these items, along with a four-pack of toilet paper rolls (becoming a real luxury!), he added to his backpack. He then left the premises for the adjacent building, a restaurant, judging from the sign in front: "Alexis' Mediterranean Food."

What's in a name? Why not *cuisine* instead of *food*? *Cuisine* is more highbrow; *food* is no-nonsense blue collar. *Alexis* is a Greek name, but the owner/chef/staff opted not to be limited to Greek fare alone, to appeal to a broader clientele. In the year following college graduation, with the encouragement (and subsidy) of a well-heeled uncle, Crow had rewarded himself with a 10-month trip to Europe, and one of the highlights had been his stay in *Ellas*, Greek for their homeland. In that short time, he'd cultivated a real attachment for the local fare.

Approaching the partially detached front door carefully so as to minimize his noise, he fantasized a smiling maitre d' waiting to show him to a table. He was hard-pressed to keep from conjuring platters of lamb kebobs, fried calamarakia, mousaka, olive oil-drizzled salads of tomatoes, cucumbers, onions, feta, and the omnipresent olives, to be washed down with retsina, followed by coffee and baklava, or maybe crema caramela... The thought of it made his mouth water; he was by no means starving but the sheer act of survival had imposed an austerity on his tribe that, in the intervening year, he had not yet gotten used to. *It must be mid-morning already*, he thought; *quit dawdling!*

Instead of a friendly wait staff, he was greeted by overturned tables, chairs, pictures and other decorations pulled from the walls—pretty much as expected. The place had experienced disgruntled guests, doubtless during the melt down. The kitchen hadn't fared much better. Though not well lit owing to just two near-ceiling windows, he was able to make out a large upright refrigerator, doors agape, stripped of contents. Next to it, the stove; opposite, a long steel counter with a double sink. Random broken crockery, glassware. All the surfaces were covered with dust along with rodent droppings; here and there, broken or bent cutlery, soiled towels. A rat's nest in one of the drawers.

On impulse, he opened the oven door to discover the first real score of his outing. Near the back on the lower rack of the dark cavern, he extracted a stainless five-quart pot, some unidentifiable residue glue-dried in the bottom. Such items were in short supply and, once cleaned up, would be prized. He located the large serving spoon, fork and spatula set and, not finding anything else worth packing, Crow wrapped the lot in towels from the previous apartment to minimize rattling, placed them carefully in his backpack, and proceeded on to his ostensible destination, the local *TruValue Hardware*.

Another trashed entryway; *We'll see what's "truly valuable" in this post-apocalyptic establishment, won't we?* Some vandalism but shelving mostly intact. What goods they held were frivolous or irrelevant: assorted models of vacuum cleaners and accessories, cleaning and polishing materials, a whole row of various paint and sealant products in pint, gallon, and five-gallon containers. He grabbed a couple quarts of water sealant and a handful of brushes. And the paint? *Maybe someday*, he thought; he'd make a note.

In an area that had once displayed bicycles, now nothing. No, wait; on a side rack, were a few tires. *Too big/bulky!*, Crow thought, spying two shelves of small rectangular boxes. Tire tubes. *Now, those are worth packing.* Small, more portable, they could have other uses. Off to one side, a tire pump and a tube-patch kit; in they went. Meanwhile, he took out the notepad and pencil from the side pocket of his rucksack, now starting to show some girth, and wrote down the data on the amount and types of paint, as well as quantity, size, and make of the bike tires. You never knew. Then, he tied the tires together and began to locate a place to stash them out of sight. His tribe had a few bikes. They were, in this post-petroleum age, the fastest, most efficient means of transporting a person with a small amount of goods, over moderately smooth terrain: mostly the formerly busy streets and congested highways. Even if his group's bikes were in serviceable condition, their tires would eventually wear out. Additionally, they could have trade value with other tribes.

Looking down the building-material aisle, he could see that the shop had been scavenged by at least one group with a specific agenda; there were virtually no nails, no fasteners, no screws to be had. The hand tool aisle had fared no better; everything of utility had already been taken. He came up with a couple pair of leather workgloves on the floor amidst the broken, trampled-on goods, but without the fine-toothed-comb treatment, there didn't appear to be much else. Working his way out, he came across a dumped-over wire display with a number of seed packets still attached, about half and half flowers and vegetables. *Why were these overlooked?* he wondered.

Each clip held from one to four packets of garden vegetables: several kinds of squash, tomatoes, onions, beets, and varieties of lettuce, cucumber, and eggplant. This, too, was a coup; he stopped counting and stuffed them all in his pack. Giving the flowers a once over, he noticed the marigolds—weren't they supposed to repel harmful insects naturally? *They don't take up any room to speak of; in they go.*

On a whim, he stood on a chair to see the hidden reaches of the upper shelves of the storage room in back and was immediately rewarded: barely within reach was an unopened cardboard carton of 20 individual boxes of twelve-each Ball regular canning lids. He took down the carton and, not finding a better place of concealment, slung the set of bike tires into its place. If he and his tribe were going to survive future winters, they would have to raise, harvest, process, and preserve most of their food. Canning fruit and vegetables, especially before rural electrification, had been one of the easiest ways to preserve surplus garden goods for the winter, spring, and early-summer months. But the Achilles heel of the canning process was a supply of steel lids; the jars were theoretically infinitely reusable, as were the steel doughnut screw-tops, but the lids were one-time use only. This discovery would provide the tribe a small cushion for canning perhaps into the following couple

21

of years or so.

Before taking leave, he caught sight of a short-handled scoop shovel propped in the shadow of the backdoor cracked ajar, doubtless forgotten by previous "shoppers." A lucky find, such a discovery was a real coup. A compact, efficient means of excavation, this one was still virginal; he'd gladly carry it. He poked his head out the back door and, after a brief pause looking for movement/listening for unusual sounds, stepped out into the bright sunlight. He took three steps toward some nearby ferro-concrete cover, having just about adjusted to the bright, shadow-less early afternoon, when he heard a sharp cry, *Hey!*

Crow reflexively crouched behind an abandoned car and looked in the direction the call had come. Two men were starting to separate as they approached him from some 50 feet away. As quiet as he'd tried to be, these guys, in the vicinity on their own agenda, must have heard Crow and investigated. He knew he had that .38 pistol in an outside pocket of his bag but he thought better about groping around for it now. He feigned nonchalance, like he might have projected the year previously on encountering unknown young adults—respectful but wary. Facing them as he slowly stood up, *Whazzup?*

The two men stopped 15 feet away. Closer, he could

see they, too, carried packs, although theirs were empty or nearly so. The older one on the right said, *That's my shovel...*

How do you figure?

Because I found it first and was just now coming back for it.

Well, slowly, stretching out the delivery, *as far as I'm concerned, I found it first.* Crow glanced from side to side looking for an escape route. Nothing looked very promising. Meanwhile, the quiet kid on the left was starting to look antsy, beyond predicting. *Whaddya say we work out somesort of a "joint ownership" agreement?*

With that shot-in-the-dark stroke, he'd broken the ice. Scarcely able to repress a smile, the ponytailed, straggly-bearded, late-30s/early-40s man on the right said, *Sure, we'll go for that. But we get first turn at our joint ownership.*

Crow barely hesitated before recognizing his best chance lay in giving up the shovel. These two guys didn't appear armed but even using the shovel as a weapon or a means of defense, he probably couldn't prevail against them in the end. And the contents of his pack? He didn't want to risk getting beat up or killed in defending his gleanings. Better to cultivate an amicable connection with these guys. Taking a step towards the older guy, shovel outstretched, he said, *Where're you guys from?*

Out east of here. You?

Everyone froze while they listened intently to a quick succession of shots in the distance to the southwest, a short interval and two more shots. When no more shots seemed forthcoming, Crow said, *Up the valley a ways.* Vague was good. Keeping specifics to oneself made sense with strangers. You could speak in general terms and still gather a lot of information. He was aware that while he was assessing them, gauging the level of tension in the interaction, as well as the overall well-being of these two, he was likewise being read, especially by the older one. Establishing identities was probably a good idea, he thought; make it personal. On the assumption that it's harder to kill someone you're on a first-name basis with, he offered, *I'm Crow; what're your names?*

Deacon; most folks call me Deke. Nodding toward the kid, dismissively, *He hasn't been with us very long—he doesn't have a name yet. How many you got in your tribe?*

Fourteen of us made it through the worst of the winter but recently we've grown some. What about you?

Eight in my group survived the winter from 11 starting out last November. In the last month, we pooled resources with two other group fragments. We're 16 nowadays. Studying the distended pack, *You find anything interesting?*

Nothing special. Odds and ends from a couple of apartments up the street. Some blankets and sheets, a pair of gloves and some seeds from inside there. A cooking pot. The briefest pause, then, *So when do I get a crack at our joint-ownership shovel?*

Deacon glanced at the shovel before returning to examine Crow. The silence was beginning to be palpable when he said, *I'll tell you what, meet me here in three months—what's that, mid-July? Say, mid-day—and I'll hand it over.*

Deal! Now gentlemen, if you don't mind, I should be moving on, Crow stretching before picking up his pack, taking his time, trying not to show nervousness/eagerness to get away. *Your tribe gotta name?*

The Rolling Stones. You?

Nothing nailed down; we're trying River Rats on for size. Extending his right hand to Deacon, *Alright Deke-of-the-Rolling-Stones, see you back here for the July powwow.*

Deacon took his hand, making eye contact congenially. Not Yet Named, the 16, maybe 17-year-old kid, gave him a vacuous stare, unresponsive to the proffered hand; not recognizably hostile, more, affectively not *there*, lacking in any emotion. *Now there's a rough transition,*

25

thought Crow.

Without looking behind him, Crow strode two blocks perpendicular from the course he'd taken, before turning back in the direction of the subway line. At the corner, he allowed himself a quick look back, reassuring himself he wasn't being followed.

* * * * *

Sparrow stirred and slowly came awake. Someone coming in, or going out more likely, had closed the door, scraping the lower edge on the sill—a minor structural flaw that, while not loud, was nonetheless audible to one not fully asleep. As she got up and dressed in the sodden early light, she tried to piece together the features of the dream just interrupted. Another episode of her life *Before*, except in exaggerated and fantasized form, of course. Something about the comfort, security, and sublime predictability of her life *then*, the halcyon days.

In her dream, the human drama seemed less important than the ease and comfort of her former life: A heated apartment with a nudge of the thermostat, a well-lighted room with a flick of a switch. The extravagant luxury of an unrestricted hot shower. A panapoly of musical choices, by the recognized-definitive musicians, via flawless

26

acoustics—at the touch of a button. A refrigerator and cupboards well stocked with her desired foods, regardless of the season. Within a few blocks in any direction, an unending cornucopia of domestic and exotic foods from far-off lands—fresh, canned, frozen, dried, juiced, or powdered —many essentially ready to ingest: *Open container. Insert contents in mouth. Chew, swallow. Repeat.*

She had been in her final year as an education major at the local university. There was a boyfriend, Lenny, she'd felt good about without needing, or even wanting, to institutionalize the relationship; there'd be plenty of time for that, wouldn't there be? *Wouldn't there?*

The days were getting noticeably longer, and while there wasn't much change in rainfall, frosts were behind them. The days between the storms were becoming balmy with the alder and maple starting to leaf out, though still chilly enough these early mornings to layer up. She left Amanita still sleeping in the women's dormitory and, in one of several pairs of rubber boots stationed near the doorway, stepped into a light drizzle.

Too familiar in the Pacific Northwest, the sky can go weeks in unrelenting weep mode; rain, in some form, is a fundamental part of the landscape. Rain nourishes life and washes away/flushes (superficially, at least) many of humanity's sins. Rain accounts for the abundance of lush green growth, as it creates lakes and rivers, running water never far away. All this was well known to every inhabitant of the region. Nevertheless, grousing about the danksoggy chillywet of it all was an important aspect of socialization; it constituted a regional pastime. Curiously, in the old days, visitors from arid regions would sometimes exhibit signs of alarm by the onset of rain. As if they were water soluble and just might dissolve into the earth, a pile of wet clothes all that remained.

Sparrow was born and grew up in the Pacific Northwest and never experienced another climate for any length of time; like most locals, she wasn't fond of getting soaked by the rain, but she wasn't particularly put out by it, either. She ducked quickly into the nearby privy before heading for the main house. It was her turn to kindle a new fire in the wood stove, the nexus of the day's early activities. In addition to warming up the main house, she needed to begin preparing a batch of quick-bread biscuits or some other starchy meal, and start heating a kettle for tea and a large pot for washing/bathing. Soon Yumi would be along to help.

Thanks to the food stocks the early group had accumulated before the Crash, and lucky acquisitions last summer and fall, the tribe had enough flour, meal, beans, and whole grains to make it through this spring and, with careful management, well into the summer. Truth to tell, however, it had been a real struggle to prepare this variety of dried grains/legumes in palatable forms. They had plenty of salt, but the sweeteners were all but gone. As for the real exotics, coffee was effectively extinct; what little remained was under lock and key, reserved for Special Occasions. Chocolate had long since been exhausted. Late last summer the newly settled group had literally reaped their hard-earned gardening reward and everyone had been in a frenzy to salt, pickle, smoke, ferment, dry, and/or can the bounty.

The winter squashes were gone by Christmas, as were the remaining potatoes, carrots, and onions. By late winter, disgruntled over their lack of stored gardening efforts, they resolved to build a better root cellar come summer and grow more beets, turnips, potatoes, onions, garlic, and carrots. Nearly everything else that had lasted this long was straight-ahead grain or legume carbohydrates which, of course, had sustained them at a basic, metabolic level. To be sure, at that level, they were humbly grateful. They quickly came to appreciate textural differences, however, the flavor and aroma variations. They'd saved till now the dried fruit and berries, as well as dried mushrooms, for the time when most other nutritive and/or flavorful additions had played out.

Among the several successful crops they'd grown,

perhaps the most underrated had been the couple of bushes of Thai hot peppers. Underrated no longer. Despite eating some fresh, chopped and stir-fried, or mixed in casseroles early on, they were able to harvest in mid-autumn as much as three dried quarts which, when ground, added an important zip to the inedible-short-of-starving; a significant pizazz to please-don't-make-me-eat-that. These few taste directions had come to be their culinary salvation. Underlying these rather peripheral concerns, however, was the growing awareness that their second winter was going to be very different from the one now slowly releasing its grip. Different and wholly dependent on this summer's harvests...

Getting a fire going each morning was made easier by the provision of the raw materials by the young folks of the tribe: dried cedar shavings; thin-split sticks of cedar, preferably, but fir or almost anything else would serve, as long as they were dry; and finally, a ready supply of bigger-but-not-too-big chunks to keep the fire going—the firebox of a wood cookstove is long enough but quite small in height/width. Unless seriously injured or sick, it had been the unfailing duty of the *juvies* to provide at least the next couple of days' firewood, rendered in appropriate form, and dry enough to support combustion. Another thing this rotating contingent of young men and women (the juvies) was responsible for was grinding the requisite amount of the specified grain by noon of the previous day, as per the chief cook's order, in their countertop-mounted hand grinder.

Sparrow had just gotten the fire going when Yumi appeared, waking and moving slowly, languidly, like a cat. *There you are! OK, water detail first: top off the tea kettle and get it heating, then fill up this 3-gallon soup pot for washing.* From dishes to bodies to clothes, washing was a compulsory part of daily activities.

A pitiable groan, uttered for effect, then attention to the task. Now 17, Yumi was still vaguely disappointed her teenage fantasies had gotten so abruptly attenuated. She was a dues-paying, card-carrying member of her lower-middle-class, inner-city high school generation, and even at 15, she'd managed to whet several of those fantasies. But now, *this*. On a rational level, she understood that *that* life was gone for good. That her expectations of the previous life—that the wanton, self-absorbed level of consumption should continue at the same pace indefinitely—were based on false pretenses; she got it. And even knowing she was fortunate to be alive and in a tribe where people took care of each other, Yumi could not resist expressing, in her own *faux*-adult way, regret at being denied several more years of narcissistic indolence. Needless to say, many more-

31

experienced, mature, mainstream citizens of at least the two previous generations, right up to the Crash were her role models for the descent into wanton consumption, she would be quick to point out. It was *the* Dominant Narrative, for crissake.

And keep that firebox stoked, Sparrow said, merely acting out her role. With few exceptions, the general rule for social interactions was "Youngers defer to Olders," with the small core of Elders having the final say. Both Sparrow and Yumi understood this very well; this wasn't a case in which the <u>Altern/Sub-altern</u> status was being contested. Sparrow was not a hard taskmaster; she was fair and had a sense of humor. It was, in fact, Sparrow's responsibility to teach Yumi how to organize the kitchen and prepare a meal for the household. Yumi was apprentice to Sparrow, and every other adult cook in turn—mostly women, but occasionally men—like pretty much everything else, on a three-day cycle.

Like Sparrow, Yumi rotated through virtually every other task, chore, or activity including sex. This pair system was the brainchild of the elders early on, Chance in particular. The genius of it was that (almost) every task was performed in minimal units of two. Partners kept alternating so that no two people spent more than two days together before they rotated to different partners. The

Elders claimed this was the quickest way for everyone in the tribe to impart and receive information/meaning/mutual appreciation with everyone else in the shortest amount of time, and thence ongoing. The central benefit this policy afforded was to promote tribal identity, and to minimize the development of factions. Within expected gyrations, the system worked pretty well.

The previous night, Sparrow had added warm water to a large pan of 10 cups of ground cornmeal, 4 cups of finely ground wheat, stirred the lot, and added more water until it was the consistency of a thick slurry; then she placed the pan in the oven to stay warm. This she now removed and examined, and again dragged a mixing spoon through the gruel. It had absorbed the water and thickened over night, as expected. She wished she could add some chopped sausage, perhaps cooked in olive oil, and a little grated Parmesan cheese; this could be a classy dish! Instead, she'd add some ground-up, dried chilies and sage from their garden, and a little salt, then spoon it into bread pans and bake it for at least an hour, depending on how hot they could get the oven.

Nobody complained. Except Yumi, of course, but that wasn't really complaining. That was more likely acting out the prerogative of a young woman between the ages of

12 and 20, Sparrow mused. As a function of the way things were *Before*? The oldest of the youths, Meadow, at 12, might just be salvageable from having imprinted on that former lifestyle as normal and desirable, and they had high hopes for Diana, their wood nymph, their child princess. Tad should be fine.

Everyone had lost weight; in Sparrow's case, through this last chaotic year, without a scales, she guessed she'd lost a good 25 lbs., and, at 5'7", 132 lbs., she was not what you'd've called pudgy a short 12 months ago. Everyone was eating less and "exercising" more, a guaranteed lose-lose in terms of weight. Now, they were getting 14 to 1600 calories each per day, they reckoned, not much above survival rations.

Up to a year ago you could have gorged on carbohydrates from an unimaginable array of sources; you could've made yourself sick from eating so much, and even though everybody understood this connection, increasing numbers of people year by year did just that. Both in the sense of binge overeating resulting in disgorgement, and in the sense of chronic overeating yielding higher probabilities of a whole litany of diseases, did people willingly corrupt themselves.

Now, well, the heavy ones seemed to have had the hardest time, and the two they'd lost over the winter, Vic and Beverly, had started with the most "insulation" at the outset. Too drastic a change, too big a shock? Who knew? It was clear there's a wide range of adjustments in adapting to a new and different environment. Some people rolled with the changes and figured out how to fit anew; others shriveled and withered—psychically speaking—at the prospect. Bev, at least, seemed to approximate the latter.

In Vic's case, he took about a month to figure out he didn't want to live without his wife and soul mate of 15 years. During that month, as he withdrew, virtually everyone engaged him, embraced him, and tried to cheer him up, which, knowing the intent, he always bore stoically. He *did* appreciate the warmth from the well-wishers, but with Bev gone, there really wasn't any way to cheer him up. In the end, the warmth and collegiality wasn't enough: he too left their company in time for Happy Thanksgiving.

With the corn pone/polenta in the oven and water heating, the two women had a chance to sit for awhile, adding wood to the firebox every few minutes. Sparrow took the initiative, *What's goin' on? You holding up?*

Yeah, I guess so. Pause, *It's a big change, that's all.*

It sure is, girl, harder on some than others. Anything in particular? You know, everybody likes you. Especially the boys, it looks like.

Sparrow pretended not to notice while Yumi blushed

and smiled faintly. She had to admit, she was a popular sex partner. *No, not really,* she said. That she wanted to talk about, anyway. She'd had sex a handful of times in her life *Before*. Furtively, in great complementary arousal, sometimes lying on their bed of clothes on the ground and, yes, in the backseat of cars. But this arrangement was several nights a week, every week, cycling among 8 or 9 horny guys, a different partner regularly, and completely sanctioned, in fact relied upon, by the tribe. Her name, pronounced "YOU-me," was the result of her *nisei* Japanese mother's attempt at preserving a semblance of her cultural roots. But owing to her willingness to pursue sexual inventiveness, some of the young bucks had taken to referring to her as "Yummy," a variation she no longer balked at.

For her part, Sparrow enjoyed making sure her sexual partners were sheathed by rolling the rubber over the agitated member herself. She never tired of feeling the nervous anticipation, the warmth of it, marveling at its growth, and the knowledge that this essential part of the man would soon be inside her.

The lopsided gender disparity—four or five sexually active women compared to eight or nine sexually active men, depending on whether Chance wanted to get laid, empowered women to have a prevailing influence on sexual policy. The system they had today—this mid-April morning —was at least the third permutation, a fine tuning, of sexual practice since a semi-stable group got established before the Crash. Since then, everyone had recognized that their whole social construct was an experiment on how to survive collectively. They were going to have to stay adaptable.

* * * * *

Notes from the journal taken by Waymer (formerly *Waymore Bently II*), recently chosen by Tribal Council as principle Scribe of the River Rats, begun this January 12th.

A couple of years ago Chance, Gaia and her kid, Coho, Blue, me, and some other folks pooled their money when it still had value in the old Petroleum Economy and bought this property. It was this act, along with stockpiling food and tools, resulting from the prescience that something like a major societal unraveling would occur, that, the rest of us realize, literally saved our lives. This house and couple of out-buildings were pre-existing structures that we've converted to our purposes. We managed to build a men's dormitory, additionally, before the Collapse.

Our tribal demographics: 11 males, 7 females.

Diana, 7; Meadow, 12; Yumi, 17; Flora, 19; Swallow, 25; Amanita, 31, pregnant, due in summer; Gaia, 44, mother of Meadow.

Tad, 9; Owl, 15; Tooloose, 16; Paco, 19; Martel, 22; Coyote, 29; Crow, 33; Waymer, 36; Blue, 43; Coho, 49; Chance, +/- 60.

1/17: I'll attempt a brief inventory of the Tribe's hardware and supplies, the result of that pre-Crash group's forethought: A 55-gallon steel drum of #1 grade kerosene for the lamps, several gallons of cooking oil, 6~8 3 lb. cans of coffee—anathema to the barrista coffee connoisseurs, but in canned form it would keep for a long time, as opposed to the fresh-roasted, bagged variety, which was good for a matter of weeks before starting to turn stale. Initially, we had a pretty good supply of dried grains and legumes, a couple of five gallon buckets full of sugar, eco-friendly clothes-washing soap, several cartons of book, as well as stick matches, a couple of 40 lb. salt blocks, a 50 lb. bag of rock salt for preserving foods, as well as 10 lbs. each of pepper and table salt; you know, logical things, though some, at this point in the winter, might wonder why more canned goods had not been stocked.

    We keep the fuel and firewood in a woodshed off to

the side of the house. Most of the rest of the stores are kept in one of the first floor back rooms, the varying amounts of grains/legumes were stored in sheet-steel-lined wood bins: wheat, rice, and corn, but also millet and rolled oats; nuts and various beans and peas. This room is also the armory, the weapons cache; it is considered off limits unless there is specific purpose, always attended in pairs at minimum. Our weapons inventory includes a 12-gauge pump shotgun, 3 boxes of shells; 3 lever or bolt action "deer rifles" of different calibers, 2~4 boxes of cartridges each; a sleek little Glock 9 mm handgun with, maybe, 70~80 rounds; a couple of crossbows with at least a hundred aluminum-shaft arrows; and, by a coup of dubious means, Mikhail T. Kalashnikov's contribution to global mayhem and destruction; for 60 years, *the* weapon of choice by revolutionaries from Central and South America to Africa; from the hill tribes along the Afghan/Pakistan border, to the jungles of the Philippines, to the squalid refugee camps of the PLO: The people's weapon, our very own AK 47, with +/- 250 rounds of ammo. Oh, yeah, and Alfred Nobel's initial claim to fame: Dynamite, 20 sticks of it (NOT stored in the house).

The kitchen and living room have been converted into one open space; with the provision of a large header spanning 16', the interior wall disappeared. The other back room, utilized as love nest at night, makes up the first floor. Under the eaves, two rooms oppose each other at the top of the stairs. One is our second nuptial chamber/screw room (*I have been enjoined to keep a "dignified" account*). The other is the tribe's office, where records, legal documents, and this journal are kept—and where Chance usually sleeps.

1/21: In what must have been one of the more bizarre of choices of advance purchases, Chance had managed to stockpile several gross of condoms. At a wholesale discount, of course. As a result, the women have been encouraged to insist on condom use—on threat of withholding sex. With one baby on the way this August, everyone understands the importance of precluding more pregnancies, not to mention STDs, for the foreseeable future. Just providing enough food for ourselves through the next year will take careful planning, based on sketchy knowledge, and even less experience—and a lot of luck. No logic could justify inviting another mouth to feed.

The women are also encouraged to make sure the men bathed; the common way they accomplish this is to wash themselves and each other simultaneously—to save precious hot water, of course, but the inherent sensuality is the unspoken draw. Overt displays of exclusive affection are discouraged but there is, nonetheless, covert compeition among the young bucks for female special attention. Women are expected to provide the bedding; it follows them wherever they sleep, from the women's dormitory to whichever room they are allotted for privacy with a man. Women take charge of washing their dual-function bedding as well as their own clothing, whereas the men have to wash, or negotiate for washing, only their own clothes and bedding.

At first the main house had only one room for these liaisons, but pressure to use it forced an early conversion of a coveted second room to a nuptial chamber. Lately, both have been occupied virtually every night. Not that couples don't hook up outside their nights together in a bedroom. Assigned partners during the course of their task, out of sight of the others, have chances to put things together, but the consensus is it doesn't happen so often. After weeks and months of this free-and-open sexual arrangement, much of the novelty has worn thin; besides, a man can virtually count on an all-night bedroom with a woman he's been getting to know pretty well via every other aspect of the tribe up to four nights a week.

1/23: There being fewer women, they have virtually no gaps beyond the standard routine of three days with one or another sleeping partner, three days without. Needless to say, they are encouraged to sign up more often, and from time to time, they do. Sometimes they sign up for the "companionship" option and surprisingly, they usually get takers. Of course, neither the woman nor the man can alter this rotation and choose his/her partner for the night. It turns out this last little item can take some getting used to.

Take Lenny, for instance. He and Sparrow came here together late last summer. They were invited to stay a couple of nights as guests. The group was smaller then, but a version of our serial sex practice was occurring. Lenny's first thought was, *What? Sex with all these foxy babes on a regular basis? Sign me up!* Then, that thought gradually gave way to his second thought: *Wait a minute! That means Sparrow is gonna be fucking every one of these guys. And they make it sound like I'd be just another guy in line, as far as Sparrow's concerned. That can't happen; we're outta here.*

Except that Sparrow had sized up the survival potential with our group compared to what she was beginning to see with Lenny under these adverse conditions. In private, she patiently-but-emphatically told him she was staying. She got her suitcase and a small bag of personal things, intent on trying out the women's dorm. By the next morning Lenny had taken their car, along with the rest of their common possessions, a fresh-baked loaf of bread intended as breakfast for the whole family, and a brush-cutting machete left on the front porch. He left with maybe half a tank of gas—good for 120 miles, give or take. Bye bye, Lenny.

2/10: Gaia is a handsome woman; at just 44, she is the tribe's oldest, and has held up well against the physical rigors of this life. A hospital RN for nearly two decades, her insights and experience have proven her value to the tribe over and over again. As in other tasks, she is still a vigorous and active sex partner, despite a curious and awkward dynamic growing between Gaia and her 12-year-old daughter, Meadow. Diana, at 7, and Meadow both are absolutely off limits for anything sexual—as is Tad, for that matter. But Meadow listens to the talk, watches the flirting and the touching, and is starting to play up her onset of puberty. In peremptory mode, the tribal council has made it clear that any man found guilty of having sex with any of these young'uns would be banished from the tribe—after first having surrendered his testicles.

Tad is short for Tadpole. The tribe adopted him early on. Dark eyes and shaggy, deep-brown hair, he's a playful and good-natured sprite with a vivid imagination, given he was orphaned/abandoned and starving when discovered, just another refugee from the Collapse. He came with some

43

fittingly pretentious name like Gabriel, Jeremiah, or Joshua, one of those big *mucky mucks* from the Old Testament. Those who knew at one time, pretend not to know now, and even though whatever moniker he'd started with had a passable shortened form, he picked up Tad from unknown quarters and it quickly caught on. Since it was never applied as a pejorative, he didn't take it as such; at nine, he doesn't know any different. By the time he might start to object, he will be perfectly capable of renegotiating a new name. *Negotiate*, because it matters not what you insist on being called, it's what the others decide to call you —with or without the consent of the so-named. Hence, Tad it is, for now.

Owl, our precocious man-child at 15, our three-eyes. Severely near-sighted, in need of thick-lensed glasses since he was four. In a freak accident, he broke the corrective lens to his dominant eye, with no back-up set. Now he alternates between wearing his one-good-lens glasses with a patch over the unaided eye—or without any aid at all, which in unfamiliar surroundings, is not much better than groping. By his own choosing, he remains at or near home where he has become the de facto house manager/major domo/comptroller.

2/12: Paco was not quite feral when the tribe took him in.

Always on the periphery, normal socialization was probably never part of his world. He heard what went on, and he understood; you could tell by how he followed the speaker. Terminally shy, if that explains anything. Hangs back, keeps a low profile, chooses not to speak in public—*public* constituting three or more folks together. Otherwise, he is completely reliable, willing to cooperate with any member on any task. At 19, he is an enthusiastic participant in the sexual rotation; some of the women find it kind of exotic-bordering-on-kinky that he rarely talks, even in such intimate circumstances.

Coyote is an original member, but, like Paco, he tends not to have a lot to say in group situations. He hails from New Orleans (pronounced "N'AWluns"), part of the Hurricane Katrina diaspora who never went back. Like the Pac man, keeps a low profile; his loyalty is not compromised by a lack of participation in the throes of policy construction.

Amanita's pregnancy is about 5 months along and while she's stayed in the sex rotation up to now, she's starting to show a bigger abdomen and, feeling more matronly, is tapering off frenetic sexuality. Instead of a three-night stint, she's more apt to do two nights, or even just one, and declare the others companionship nights, no sex; or spend the other nights in the women's dorm. Which

45

leaves a gap that can stay vacant, unless an unoccupied woman decides to fill in. It goes without saying that preferences develop over time; this is probably inevitable. But one is not able to jigger the assigned pairing simply because one is experiencing a special attraction for a particular individual, or sidestep the designated person because of a personal disagreement. You don't get to finagle out of spending the night with someone; however, the basic rule is, no one is required to have sex with anyone else.

2/17: Yeah, right; not *required,* but every sexually active person understood if there were no sex parameters, as an example of all the group's standards, there would be anarchy. It's become apparent neither solitary individuals, nor couples, and maybe not even small groups could survive long in this post-petroleum environment. But, the thinking goes, somesort of group/community confederation might make it. Without knowing the optimal numbers, something like a large tribal "family" on rural, arable land with nearby running water, might be a person's best bet; time would tell. Such a tribe could not hold together except in two (and only two?) scenarios. The first is the approach we are trying: inclusive, egalitarian, that which works best for most, if not all, folks. Conflict resolution accomplished through all manner of group influence; persuasion, perhaps; coercion as a last resort, based on the decision of the tribal council, or in rare instances, the triad of elders.

The other scenario was the age-old paradigm: Might makes right; the most powerful decide the terms, their underlings enforce the rules. Sex for women under such circumstances had been and is still fundamentally brutal, nasty, and compelled under duress—at minimum, submitted to. For the man reasonably well connected, sex happened almost at will via the Jefe's castoffs or rejects. Otherwise, it was catch as catch can. One's key to survival in this latter system rested on cozying up to the Top Dog and his/her coterie—and hoping their eventual collapse wouldn't include you.

But in our system, the one we are trying to make work, sex is definitely not obligatory; both men and women occasionally exercise their prerogative to keep the night's intimacy shy of full sexual activity. And of course, what gets negotiated out of sight/earshot of others is, well, Who's to know?

Spending the night with this other person without having sex occurs when the woman is having her period, or when either is not in the mood. One avoids a foul call by signaling one's intent in advance. That way, no dashed expectations. Let's say, for example, Martel is the next guy on the list and, at a robust 24, coming off his three-day fast, he could really be looking forward to discharging mighty blasts of viscid rainbows.

However Flora, paired with him today, just experienced the vigorous onset of menses. If a substitute volunteers, then Flora could retire to the dormitory. If no substitute appears, he would stay next, first in line for sex. Or he could choose to stay with Flora as a companion. Of course, other methods of sexual expression occur via interpersonal negotiation, as was common among consenting adults in the previous social incarnation before the Fall. It's just that we've adjusted the age of adulthood slightly downward from much of the former mainstream norm. In view of our drastically altered circumstances, we are not able to indulge the juvies as long as the previous social incarnation, whereby a person was considered adult at the age of 18, in terms of full citizenship, emancipation from parents, voting, and serving in the military. In virtually every measurable way, though, such teenagers were wholly dependent on parents and the former community. With us, every person has a role to play. The juvies—even Tad and Diana—are primarily acolytes or apprentices to the older, more experienced members.

One unspoken realization dawns on each sexual person sooner or soon: everybody at the Haven would benefit from the addition of one to three females between the ages of 17 and +/-40; however, short of a better-balanced gender mix, we do pretty well. The prohibition of <u>pair binding</u> keeps us focused on the whole group, as opposed to fragments of that whole. The other reason concerns economies of resources. We have three buildings to maintain instead of eight or ten—however many couples require their own private nest. We heat, maintain, clean, etc. a men's and a women's dormitory, and the mainhouse. Our close-quarters arrangement both unites us in common cause and requires fewer resources to manage it.

This concludes a bare outline of how sex is practiced in our tribe, to help the reader navigate the tribal conventions.

<u>2/21</u>: Tribal Organization: Our emphasis is on pragmatic utilitarianism; that which tends to promote survival, that which works. The *summum bonum*. Needed skills any more comprise the criterion for acceptance of newcomers. Authority and responsibility is accorded to the most experienced/knowledgeable individual within the subset task, otherwise by seniority, which—no surprise—is often the person with most experience/knowledge. If you accept the notion that we must rely on one another, then it follows that we must all get proficient at nearly every task, we must become competent generalists, able to fill in when another

member is unable. This despite the fact that we all have likes and dislikes, dispositions toward some experiences, away from others.

Decision-making occurs via the Tribal Council, comprising all the 30-and-over adults, permits any comment on behalf of or in opposition to an issue. If after thorough discussion, 2/3 of attendants can't reach accord, then the Elders (currently 2 men, one woman) have final say, but they must all agree.

The Council meets formally every Sunday afternoon, and any other time the issue compels it, usually evenings, depending on the urgency. Since early on, the members have recognized the need of a scribe, to chronicle our major events, to document our laws, and to report the findings of these councils. I was given this honor/responsibility mid-January—half a year after the tribe began operating on this land.

Food: Stockpiled and foraged commodities, along with the first summer's garden surplus, is projected to be marginally adequate the 1st year. Even so, everyone is sick of corn variations: Corn bread, cornmeal mush, polenta, but recognize we are lucky to have come by three sacks of dried kernel corn early in the Upheaval. Other arrangements will be necessary to survive the 2nd winter. A great tragedy, chocolate is long gone, and even with coffee heavily rationed, it is fading fast. They remain the source of long-standing lamentation, the stuff of wistful memories. The kitchen committee has budgeted the black tea stash to see us through the summer. To be followed by survival without *any* caffeine? Not without pain. Abundant mint and chamomile tea from our garden provide a pleasant drink but will hardly be a substitute for coffee or chocolate.

Hygiene: We managed to install two passive solar water heater panels on the south-facing pitch of the roof, which supplement the plumbing through the giant wood stove, and into a couple of giant storage tanks—to insure enough hot water for bathing. Most of us above the teenage years live in dread of toothaches. It signals an unpleasant extraction, almost surely. We're quite attentive to all manner of cuts, bites and scratches, prepared to take on the first sign of infection with an impressive array of disinfectants, antibiotics, potions and salves—all monitored by Gaia, our resident health care expert. Garnered soap, shampoo, and detergent from the previous fall have seen us thus far, but all are running low. We need to be relearning how to make soap. In terms of coiffure: Both men and women tend toward a simple, relatively short, unisex haircut, rendered with scissors—less volume of hair translates to less water and less shampoo, a finite and dwindling resource. Shaving is a thing of the past, which includes legs and pits, as well as chins and jowls.

Turf location was decided upon nearly two years previously by 1) abundant water, arable land, 2) pre-existing structures, 3) relative isolation—need for degree of "inaccessibility" from urban centers, 4) defendability—recognizing that no place is completely impregnable. Therefore, questions are raised as to a fall-back plan to being overrun... The Council is currently undergoing a debate as to whether we should relocate to a more remote, less vulnerable homeland. Argument against, summarized: Many express widespread pain/anguish in the thought of having "wasted" our energy, leaving our considerable effort here behind, abandoning a known for an unknown quantity. Argument on behalf: If we are completely overrun here, all this will have been in vain anyway. There is, of course, no way to determine likelihood of this happening, but most acknowledge a degree of vulnerability here. In leaving, this will not have been a wasted experience; over time, we would be able to take virtually everything portable —and all our accumulated knowledge and experience—to a new, more remote and hence, safer, site. With no resolution in sight, we hope to send out some exploratory forays as the weather dries out, perhaps late Spring/early Summer.

* * * * *

By the numbers (in the months preceding the Collapse):

37th: Rank of the US for quality and comprehensiveness of health care—worst among industrialized nations

1st: Rank of the US in spending for health care—more than any other nation per capita

48,000,000, or more than 15% of the US population: Number/percent of Americans without any form of health care

$711,000,000,000: FY 2009 budget for the US military, including supplemental funding for Afghanistan and Iraq operations, all of it borrowed

$709,400,000,000: the combined 2007 military budgets, in descending order, for the next 44 countries, in billions of US$: #2 China-121.9, #3 Russia-70.0, #4 UK-55.4, #5 France-54.0, #6 Japan-41.1, #7 Germany-37.8, #8 Italy-30.6, #9 Saudi Arabia-29.5, #10 South Korea-24.6, #11 India-22.4, #12 Australia-17.2, #13 Brazil-16.2, #14 Canada-15.0, #15 Spain-14.4, #16 Turkey-11.6, #17 Israel-11.0, #18 Netherlands-9.9, #19 UAE-9.5, #20 Taiwan-7.7, #21 Greece-7.3, #22 Iran-7.2, #23 Myanmar-6.9, #24

Singapore-6.3, #25 Poland-6.2, #26 Sweden-5.8, #27 Colombia-5.4, #28 Norway-5.0, #29 Chile-4.7, #30 Belgium-4.4, #31 Egypt-4.3, #32 Pakistan-4.2, #33 Denmark-3.9, #34 Indonesia-3.6, #35 Switzerland-3.5, #36 Kuwait-3.5, #37 South Africa-3.5, #38 Oman-3.3, #39 Malasia-3.2, #40 Mexico-3.2, #41 Portugal-3.1, #42 Algeria-3.1, #43 Finland-2.8, #44 Austria-2.6, #45 Venezuela-2.6

150,000 Hiroshima-sized bombs: Equivalency of America's nuclear arsenal

$17,600,000,000: Annual cost to *maintain* America's nuclear arsenal and delivery system

 $700,000,000,000: Annual cost of America's consumption of imported oil (*Newsweek*, 8/25/08)

$16,000,000,000, last among developed nations: America's foreign aid, in proportion to its GDP

One-twentieth, or 5%, and shrinking: Ratio of US population to Earth's human population

One-quarter, or 25%: Percentage of US consumption of Earth's resources

$10,200,000,000,000: The debt owed by US citizens to themselves—and increasingly, to foreign stakeholders

$1,600,000,000,000: The debt Americans owe to the increasingly restive People's Republic of China, and mounting at the rate of about $1 billion per day

2,250,000: the number of people in US prisons (in 2006). At 751: 100,000 population, the highest ratio in US history and highest in the world. The next six, ranked in descending order, are Libya, 217:100 K; Iran, 212:100 K; UK, 148:100 K; China, 119:100 K; Canada, 107:100 K; and France, 85:100 K.

251~248,000,000 years ago: the Permian Extinction in full collapse. 95% of all marine species and over 70% of terrestrial vertebrate species died out in "the greatest mass extinction in Earth's history."

1950~2050(?) CE: Triggered by disruptions from global climate change, and unsustainable pressure put on a global range of biologic habitats by *Homo sapiens*, Earth is poised to experience the greatest mass die off since the Permian Extinction, bringing to a dramatic end the absurdly short-lived Anthropocene Epoch.

PART II

Give me a job, give me security
Give me a chance to survive
I'm just a poor soul in the unemployment line
My god I'm hardly alive
My mother and father,
my wife and my friends
I see them laugh in my face
But I've got the power and I've got the will
I'm not a charity case...

> *Blue Collar Man,*
> Styx

On a whim, Chance nosed his beat-up Subaru into the parking lot of Tiny's Tavern, the neighborhood watering hole. Occasionally, he'd stop off for an hour or two of departure-from-the-routine for a drink and a casual examination of the clientele. He was no longer trolling for lonely ladies; he was of an age when waning hormones had released some of their grip, which was, frankly, a bit of a relief after decades—not just most of, but *all* of his adult life; it was an important aspect of how he had identified himself—in thrall of sex. Oh, the drive was still there; it just occupied a back seat as opposed to the primary, driving role anymore. Increasingly, he considered himself a student of human behavior without a particular agenda, a kind of amateur behavioral psychologist, if you will: What, on God's green earth, made folks do the tragic and bizarre things they did; what made 'em *tick*?

It was a typically cold, soggy evening. *Winter in the Pacific northwest; what the hell did you expect,* he muttered. Still, knowing it was typical didn't ease the dank, omnipresent-clammy feeling. The depressives and their ilk had mercifully managed to survive the maniacal holiday season with its forced gaiety and obligatory consumption, but the doldrums of late January were to be endured in an unrelievably dreary level of hell. Finding a warm, reasonably well-lit room with "live entertainment"—the customers—while he copped a booze buzz, would serve as an antidote.

Or at least a distraction.

Mid-week and a slow night; that suited Chance fine. One of the three pool tables in the back provided the superficial focus of a threesome; two similarly dressed guys vying for the attention, if not the exclusive approval, of the well-proportioned late-20s brunette, clearly the focus of the construction workers—the 9-ball game was a flimsy pretext. Other groupings occupied no more than half the booths. A couple at the end of the bar were into at least their third or fourth round of drinks, taking their time getting comfortable with each other as a prelude to relocating to one-or-the-other's domicile with carnal intent. The Sonics and Blazers were battling it out on the screen over the bar, volume barely audible. Mid-bar, head bowed, staring at nothing, oblivious to the game, a moderately disheveled late-thirties/early-forrties man slouched.

Drunk, most likely. Maybe in the midst of something, thought Chance. He nodded to the bartender and took a stool respectfully a couple removed from the catatonic. He ordered a gin and tonic and had a better look around the room. Judging from the raised voices and slurred speech, the folks from the booth back by the pool tables were adequately into their cups; otherwise the place was quiet. When his drink arrived, he ventured, *Bloozers up by 12?! What planet is this?* Chance was ambivalent about sports, even when it came to the local team, but he scanned the sports pages of the local rag regularly to get a sense of what other people thought was significant, in order to make small talk.

The tall, wiry barkeep, an adept at the art of verbal shit-slinging himself and able to see it coming from 10 paces, fed the conversational flame but barely: *Yeah, but it's only the 3rd quarter; they got lotsa time to throw it away*, and moved on to other tasks.

Apparently the repartee had roused his neighbor from his stupor. Chance was replacing his glass to the coaster when he noticed the man giving him a deadpan look. *You a fan?* Chance inquired, thumbing at the screen. After an uncomfortably long time, the man slowly blinked his eyes and shook his head. *Me either. Just tryin' to make connections, like everybody else.* With no apparent response forthcoming, Chance returned to his drink and a glance at the game. In that brief interlude, the momentum of the game had turned. *Lead down to seven; startin' to slide,* he muttered to himself.

Whadju say? The man's first significant gesture of

communication, a query out of the blue, startled him.

I was saying the Bloozers' lead was down to seven— actually down to five now.

No. Before that. About making connections...

Time for some quick clarification. Time to dispel any expectations: *I meant that pretty much everybody is looking for human connection. That's all I meant. Otherwise, why drink in a public tavern, instead of the privacy of your own home. I'm straight, by the way,* offered as an afterthought.

A hint of a smile before reclouding. *Yeah, me too. What kind of human connection?*

I don't know; pretty much any kind, I guess. Hopefully positive and mutually supportive, but of course, that isn't always the way it works, is it?

Man, you got that right! Richard Pink was hours away from pulling a Hemingway, blowing his brains all over his rental garage with a borrowed 12-gauge shotgun. He'd given some thought to doing the deed in his apartment living room, but it was going to leave a big "mess" and he bore his landlord no particular ill will.

He'd been diagnosed with PTSD from two tours of duty in Iraq, where it was absolutely insane to thrust an American soldier into a completely unfamiliar culture and expect him/her to distinguish ally from enemy. He'd had to forego his natural inclination to give locals the benefit of the doubt as to their potential for posing a threat. That disposition, or something very much like it, had proven fatal for a couple of his mates, and so thereafter, for any local you didn't have a high degree of confidence in, the default position was to take 'im out. Pretty much everyone erred on the side of caution; not as commonly as Brickwater mercenaries maybe, but there was *collateral damage* and non-combatants were killed.

By the completion of his second tour, he was a skittish, jumpy, mentally-challenged discharge, programmed to perform according to military protocol, but marginally able to manage his affairs left to his own devices. In the eight months since he mustered out, he was proving to be incapable of holding down a job. Quick to anger with mindless bureaucracy, anxious in most social situations, he'd burned bridges with a steady girlfriend and all his old contacts. Family relations were already stretched to the limit, and he was loath to burdening them further.

He got nothing but a run-around at the VA hospital. He was on a list to see one of the staff shrinks. *Maybe next month*, the intake processor offered hopefully; *Oh, and fill out this form...* His credit card was maxed out, unemployment expiring. It wasn't just that life was bleak; there simply was no relief in sight. Time to call it quits.

Buzzed by the alcohol but not drunk, Richard Pink had been only too willing to spill his guts to this sympathetic stranger. For Chance, this was richer pay dirt than he'd been looking for, but he didn't shy from the dour contact. Ignoring the issue of suicide, he had eventually piqued the man's curiosity by telling him he could use his help the following day. Chance had a project that needed another perspective. First, though, he had to assure Pink he was not a Bible thumper or some other kinky do-gooder on a mission. *Depending on what we mean by "kinky do-gooder,"* he thought, *because we're all on a mission.* Furthermore, Chance agreed not to try to talk him out of offing himself, if that was what he finally decided. Would he agree to meet for breakfast, on Chance's invitation? Where was good, that place just down the road, Barney's? At 9 am? Fine. Barney's at 9, it was. What did the man have to lose, right? If he didn't like the pitch, the garage and Papa's ghost with the shotgun would be waiting.

* * * * *

Bolting the tail end of his tepid first cup of coffee by a quarter past, Chance was beginning to wonder if he'd read his evening interlocutor wrong. He was casting about for the floating coffee waitress to top him off, when the

63

tentative, somewhat sheepish Richard Pink entered and looked around the room. Chance beckoned to him, and over cheap, plentiful, fried everything, he outlined what he had in mind for the day: some land scouting. In recent months the bottom had fallen out of the housing market, owing to excessive greed on the part of real estate speculators, moneylenders of every stripe, and the raw avarice of the house buyers, buying more than they could pay for. Since the freefall of widespread corporate bankruptcies, loss of jobs, and housing foreclosures, this was bargain hunting at its best.

Chance was particularly interested in rural property for sale; hopefully, a place already improved upon, no matter how run-down or seedy. A place well removed from the city with gravity-fed water and at least the potential for cultivation. A place where a handful of people might recreate meaning and purpose in the face of a social organization bent on self-destruction.

With real estate prices in the toilet, Chance had gotten wind of a couple of parcels less than two hours from the city and within an hour of each other, plus or minus. On the way, he had time to flesh out his ideas further; this was to be a new beginning, new names included. Henceforth, Richard Pink, who was not rich in the normal sense of the word, and not suggestive of anything pink, could come up with his own new name, but in the meantime, would be called Blue, since he certainly was emotionally down.

Maybe it should be Dark Blue, Chance quipped, then quickly apologized for his tainted humor.

Happy to get out of his own head for a while with this character's far-fetched story, he was long past caring about a harmless new name. *Crazy, probably. Most likely harmless bonkers,* he thought. And, surprisingly, by humoring this guy, in tiny increments, formerly-Richard Blue began to locate *terra firma* and rediscover aspects of himself he still liked.

On the fringes, Chance's rap was plenty far-fetched. Phrases like, *Agents for change; Proactive rather than reactive; Free-range humans; Sustainability by design or by natural default; Creative chaos;* and *Agents of our own destiny* got bandied about willy-nilly. But the guy struck a familiar chord when he launched into his critique of what that Frog philosopher, Bourdieu, called "social capital"—the current narrative of life as we in the US know it, the one most of us were born into, the only one most of us know. Chance's thesis was this life, as characterized by the dominant narrative, is *insane.*

Insane, if by no other measure than sustainability.

*Un*sustainability, according to Chance, assured a drastic change, if not complete collapse. Any society that consumed its capital, the basic resources, consumed beyond the carrying capacity of the rest of the biosphere to support it, under the false and transitory delusion (coming to be dispelled by the downward slope of Hubbard's Peak, beyond the halfway point of discovery/extraction/consumption of all known petroleum reserves) that we could continue that lifestyle indefinitely—such a society was insane. Given the inescapable, increasing scarcity of petroleum and natural gas, and given our utter dependence on these fuels, without committing to immediate and fundamental change, collapse was inevitable. Any society wantonly advancing its own folly, knowing where it would lead, was textbook insane. Such a society would be committing its own offspring, those who survived, and the rest of the planet, to a far bleaker and more compromised world.

Otherwise "normal" people construct "abnormal" responses to an insane social order, Chance said to his captive audience. *At least a part of why people act out from their core identity is, I think, an attempt to establish a measure of individuality, a little personal expression, in the onslaught of pressures to be good, submissive, worker-ant consumers. People are not judged by their private thoughts, but by their actions, by how they behave, how they conform or drift from the norm. And otherwise-*

normal people acting strangely, folks behaving just a little too eccentrically as they attempt to cope with a dehumanizing environment, well, such people are made to feel abnormal—and have at times been institutionalized for their abnormalities—all according to the standards set by mainstream society, which, as we've noted, is itself, utterly delusional. "Absurd," Sartre would say, Chance said, more than a little cryptically.

The trick, according to Chance, was to reconstruct their social units in ways that would be literally sustainable. Surviving on what they could grow and raise to feed themselves. In so doing, they would discover a different potential, a positive, cooperative identity. This was beyond the Era of the Ego. Each person would be expected to discover how s/he could contribute to the well being of the whole group. For all of them, this would be a real-life learning experience with and from each other, if they were going to make it work.

Blue had taken some college before military service and had no problem following the conceptual picture Chance was painting. Had even heard of that big-shot French philosopher, although he would've been hard pressed to cite any specific insight relating to Sartre. What made his head swim was the question of whether the notion was necessary, let alone feasible, or appropriate. And while you are at it, how it might apply to him.

Ok, I'm getting the picture. What's it got to do with me?

Ah, the $64 question! It's got everything to do with you. Or nothing... your call. I was going to drive out and check on these properties today anyway. Pause for rumination. *In view of what else you had going on—that twilight between No Direction Home and Goodbye—I thought this might rouse your curiosity.*

Instinctively defensive, searching for the other person's advantage, Blue was feeling a little college-fraternity rushed. It was pleasant to be treated as an equal; he basked in having his opinion sought out, but what was the angle? *Well, you definitely got my attention. Just wondering where I might fit, is all.*

Chance nodding, *Fair enough. Why don't we keep it loose, for starters? We're coming up on this first place pretty quick. If you don't mind, stick with me and let me do most of the talking, assuming there's anyone around. Keep your eyes and ears open and we'll discuss your observations on the way out.*

The first property was suitably distant from the Interstate—some 20 miles or so. Less than a quarter mile from a well-traveled state highway, though. A definite downside, according to Chance. In a steady drizzle, they

68

skirted a long open meadow before the graveled road entered some trees. Soon, the house. The realtor said she'd try to be there but the owners understood they'd be poking around, trying to get a sense of the place. None of the vehicles looked like they'd been driven anytime recently. They had permission to peer into windows, unless someone was at home, at which time they were to be granted general access through the place.

A rap at the door; no response. *The realtors and sellers all think the buyer cares most about the house, so I usually let their house rap run its course before getting a sense of the lay of the land, the neighbors, stuff like that. Let's look around a bit.* They walked along one side of the house toward, perhaps, a storage or work shed and a barn-like structure in progress, foundation poured and half framed some months prior. From the front of this building, Chance pointed out the 4- or 5-year-old orchard and berry patch, and beside them, the pasture. *Likely these or former owners kept horses or some other hobby grazers.* Beyond the pasture in a big swath were denuded hills, here and there a substandard token hemlock, cedar, or fir standing solitary in a thicket of a ten- to twelve-foot-tall reprod (woods-speak for monoculture replanting) of less than 10 years. The owners had left some trees in and around the buildings and along the creek bottom, maybe 3 to 4 acres altogether, and stripped the rest of the 40-plus acres.

One guess is these folks coasted on the earnings from clear-cutting these hillsides 10 years ago. Money's run out, mortgaged to the teeth, time to bail. They want too much money, is the problem. One of several problems... They walked off toward the opposite side of the house; Chance wanted to see what the creek looked like in winter. *It had better be pretty robust 'cause this is the season of maximum rainfall.* Arriving at creekside: *From the lay of the land and the size of the creek, it had to've originated off this parcel some distance from here.* Muddy, it had silted up and spread out in low-lying areas; it had certainly not benefited from the clear cutting.

If Chance had been positive enough about the property's prospects, he would have insisted on walking the creek up to its source. Instead, *I've seen enough. Let's hit the road.*

Driving on to their second site, Blue got back to it. *Ok, I get that our country's facing some real problems, even that there seems to be a lack of political will to take on most of 'em. But you come across as positively unpatriotic,* feeling a twinge, a small poke at the pride he believed he was entitled to for having served his country two tours in Iraq.

I respect your service but not the purpose for which

you served, Chance said cautiously. *That was not your decision, so I bear you no ill will. But the invasion of Iraq was a colossal blunder in many respects, and will undoubtedly contribute to Merka's downfall. My assertion that national/international entities are likely to disintegrate is not a matter of patriotism. It's got nothing to do with love of country. The people will still be here, the towns, the highways. However, hospitals, police and fire protection, and libraries aren't likely to hold up, once the Collapse gets going. Just no longer any reason for, and thus no longer a mechanism for unifying any big, fat ungovernable entities, like the US of A. So I'm concentrating more of my energy on love of community rather than love of country, since I have grave doubts of our nation's survivability. The two are not oppositional, by the way; it's possible to love one's country through love of community.*

A few minutes of silence trickled by while this psychic shock wave dissipated; Blue shifted focus, *So you really think you're going to find a chunk of land out here somewhere and reinvent the country? Our country, which shows no explicit signs of disappearing? I mean,...* trailing off, not knowing how to proceed.

In short, no. All I can say is, I think we, collectively, are in for somesort of a major crash. The only real

71

question is when, and no one can answer that one. Merka's fucked, along with big chunks of the rest of the world, and I can't get it up to be all that sorry. Corporate-nation-statehood, and other power alliances, had their shot at making it better...Hell, making it work at all, except for the privileged few! Lo and behold, unchecked power yielded unlimited greed, which only made it worse! For now, I'll settle for survival. Socially, one of 18 to 26 members of a tight-knit community probably has the best chance, all things being equal. When there's some breathing room, we'll see how all who remain might get along on a bigger scale.

You know, I'm not alone in this. You could check out some list-serves online; there are lots of deeply concerned folks all over the place. Back in the city I've been talking to a few folks who are ready to commit to a project like this— pooling our money and resources to try to make a go of it. We all think it's important to act now, before the crash, while our money is still worth something. You know, anticipate rather than react. After this unraveling begins, well, all bets are off.

They drove on in silence for a time while Blue tried to make sense of it all. Finally, *I can't tell whether you're a lunatic or a prophet. There's a coherence to what you say, but it flies in the face of everything I've grown up with and based my life on. It's all very confusing...*

Yep. Two years ago, I was in the same boat. Considering mainstream society, of course, I am crazy; there's no way I'm "normal" by their standards. But I'm turning the tables on 'em, flashing a demented leer. I'll wear a lunatic badge proudly, under the present circumstances. Look, I'm not trying to twist your arm, here. All I'm saying is, give it some time. Think it through. I could be wrong, of course. Nobody's got the future down, that's for sure. Let's say, for the hell of it, I've got this whole notion of societal collapse completely bollixed, and we still go ahead and try to create a sustainable community somewhere out here on the land. Five years, ten years go by and the world invents new ways to keep chugging along, maybe making improvements as we go.

But shrinking resources, especially petroleum and natural gas, and an increasing human population are facts of life. So going "green," trying to live pay-as-you-go subsistence, is not going to be a magnitude of blunder anyone's going to be ashamed of down the road. I look forward to the time when we can slap each other on the back and have a good laugh over what fools we'd been. People aren't coerced into this, you know; anyone who opts into this plan can opt out at any time. On the other hand, what if I'm <u>right</u>? Despite all your previous

73

experience and training, what if this crackpot scheme, this twisted projection, turns out to be the way it shakes out? I wouldn't want to bet on your chances at survival if you're part of the rabble and the ugliest of these scenarios pans out...

After a pause, Chance queried, *By the way, whadju think of that property back there?*

I don't know; it looked all right to me. The house looked lived in, a couple of out buildings, a barn started, running water, like you said. Somebody must have had similar ideas as you to start the orchard and berry patch. But you hardly looked at the house.

You're right; I gave it a quick once over. My realtor/contact sent me the specs on the place online, but I wanted to see if the house was suitable as transition housing, which it is. I was more curious to see the arable land—not much there. Like you, I was impressed by the fruit tree and berry effort. But it's going to take a lot of work to bring that creek back to a healthy state, years' worth, probably. The upshot of it is, I wouldn't evaluate that parcel very highly. Maybe we'll get lucky with this next one.

The monochrome gray and constant drizzle surrendered to intermittent patches of blue sky seen among wads of wet mattress stuffing flung to the sky, a fleet of tossed gray rags, scudding across the horizon. Here and there across the wide valley the drizzle might give way to a brief, more intense squall as a passing cluster of clouds could bear the sorrow no longer, resorting to inconsolable weeping. But increasingly as they drove on, glimpses of sun penetrated the ragged patchwork of gravid clouds and such sightings were a cause for minor celebration. Slowing to track mileposts and addresses on rural mailboxes, Chance eventually found the right road leading obliquely from the state highway. They passed a couple of driveways before coming to the correct one a mile or so off the state highway at the head of a broad, partially forested valley.

This one's a little farther from the main road; a good omen for starters, Chance said. A little more, beyond the open-gated entryway, the house became visible.

That pickup's someone's run-around, Blue said. *More'n likely, someone's home this time.*

After parking the car next to the pickup, the two walked the path to the front of the gabled, two-story, traditional rural house from the '50s. Having a quick look at the grounds before reaching the porch, Chance was stunned to see four or five adult llamas in a large fenced area. *Well, I'll be damned! You know anything about llamas?*

Sorry, boss, no clue.

You s'pose people raise them to eat? And don't call

me boss.

Ok, partner. Well, what else would they be good for? hoping, reflexively, not ever to be hungry enough to have to slaughter, butcher, cook, then eat a llama. But then, Blue had never gone more than a day without food in his life; had no concept of what he would be capable of eating after, say, four days without food of any sort.

An elderly woman met them at the door accompanied by her growling canine protector, wary of the strangers but soon put at ease. Chance introduced himself and his friend to Loretta Hanson and, expecting them, she invited them in, offering tea or coffee. They accepted, and over coffee, she gave an overview of the property: The house was a three bedroom, one and a half bath, nearly 1600 sq ft, with a partial, unfinished basement. There was, of course, a mid-sized barn for hay storage and shelter for the llamas. She had an electric-pump well but there was a creek along the east side of the property; Forest Service beyond and above the property line. The old gal guessed at least 35 acres of arable land, some of which had never been cultivated. Another 20 or so in forested land.

She offered to show them the house. *If you don't mind, Mrs. Hanson, I'd like to take a look outside. Please give my friend here the indoor tour,* nodding at Blue.

Sure, I don't mind; that is, if the gentleman is

alright with the arrangement, ending the sentence on a rising tone, questioning.

It's fine by me, Blue said.

Heading for the front door, Chance said, *I promise not to monkey with anything.* Seeing the dog at the door, tail wagging, an alert mongrel with a fair amount of terrier in him, *Is it ok if your dog comes with me?*

Heavens yes! If he wants to go, then by all means. Name's Jack, by the way.

Thanks. Be back in a few. Slapping his thigh, *Come on Jack!* to the eager dog. Outside, he made a beeline to the outbuildings, starting with the pole barn. On the second floor, there was a hayloft over, perhaps, 3/4 of the ground floor. Large animal pens occupied much of the ground floor. From the back of the barn, acres of mostly open land were fenced, but it looked like a lot of the fencing was the electric variety—fine, as long as you're plugged into the grid, or could recharge the batteries. There looked to be a combination tool-and-woodshed. A ramshackle greenhouse. An older orchard, apple or pear likely, badly in need of pruning. A busy little creek gurgled and splashed along the bottom edge of the fruit trees never having to flow far without the shelter of evergreen or deciduous trees— cover from sunlight in summer, at least.

The man paused a minute to take in the overall

feeling of the place, and leaned down to stroke his companion. *Never hurts to build positive reinforcement*, he mused. An errant shower caught Chance walking back to the house. Where there'd been traffic, the ground was muddy. He stomped, then scraped his shoes at the foot of the porch. Approaching the door, he rapped a couple times, and let himself in. Blue and Mrs. Hanson were sitting in the living room, talking about the means of heating (fuel oil), and its cost (expensive and getting more so). At a lull in the conversation, Chance asked if there had been much interest in the property.

There was some early on. But the mortgage crisis kept getting worse and folks lost confidence in their ability to bear the load anymore. On top of the situation where banks wouldn't lend to them, anyway, at least these days. My Ernie gave up on life a coupl'a years back, and I've done pretty well on my own, considering. But, except for my pet llamas, I can't keep the place up. My daughters up in the city talked it over; you know, I prob'ly shouldn't be driving much anymore, so they talked me into moving up close to them so they could help me more directly, as things begin to slide for me. Can't say I'm real happy about the idea, but changes come at you anyway, ready or not. Sometimes your choices amount to the lesser of two undesirables.

What an enchanting old chatterbox, thought Chance. *And lonely as hell for a little human contact.* He told the woman he was favorably impressed with the property, that it was a sizable sum of money, and he would need to consult with his financial backing and confirm some legal issues. He had the land particulars from the realtor in town. He would contact her soon—within the next two weeks, he thought.

On the way back, the two men compared observations. Both liked what they'd seen. Blue thought the house was well cared for, and found Mrs. Hanson informative about details of her life on the property. For his part, Chance didn't know what to make of the llamas, but found the landscape to be generally suitable for their hypothetical-group purposes. After a half hour or so of light conversation, they lapsed into a comfortable silence. He turned on the radio to a classical station; an exquisite *andante*, a slow, delicate, lyrical, middle movement from a piano concerto enveloped them, eliciting a muffled *Humf!* from Blue.

Must not be a Mozart-kinda guy, Chance surmised.

Before dropping him off at his apartment, Chance got Blue to agree to meet for lunch a couple days later—an implicit understanding that suicide was relegated to a back burner, at least for the time being—then, simple farewells.

Not a bad day, all things considered.

* * * * *

He devoted the following days to researching Loretta Hanson's property: Whether she owned it outright or not, when the house had been constructed, and whether it had been permitted or grandfathered into the tax records—accepted because it was built before strict building standards were put in place. What was the zoning; were there conditions that would permit more single-family dwellings? How much were the property taxes; how much for "improvements" and how much for the land? He also wanted to check the adjoining property owners, and the topography of the area. With data in hand, he set up a meeting with Coho, a disenfranchised half-Native American, his increasingly skittish wife, Becky, Nurse Gaia and her kid, and Waymore Bentley II, an eccentric Brit of dubious motives, suspect interests, and undisclosed means.

At Coho and Becky's modest apartment he described what he'd seen at the Hanson place and what he'd learned about it since. Chance outlined the features he considered positive, primary among them, the fact that State and National Forest Services managed most of the land in the wooded, hilly country higher up behind the site. This was good because these agencies could not sell the land surrounding 2/3 of the 63-acre-Hanson spread without a lengthy public process. Otherwise, remaining in the public trust, it would continue to be looted piecemeal for its timber resources by private enterprise whenever the gettin' was good. Until the whole scheme disintegrated.

Not a great situation in the near term, but better than if some or all of it were in private hands outright. In that scenario, it would be possible to envision roads, other construction before the Collapse, and then runoff from human activity in those uplands onto the Hanson spread would cause pollution consequences long after.

Thankfully, such was not the case. Currently, the condition of the surrounding forest was pretty good: not yet significantly mature enough to be marketable—thus, not likely to be clearcut soon. Mixed conifer and native deciduous. The creek running through the place looked like it would still be substantial in the summer, but nobody could say for sure. The nearest neighbors were a couple of retirees living ½ mile downstream, creekside in a doublewide, the creek, by then, a much more significant watercourse with the addition of several other tributaries.

Other private property holdings in the area seemed to be small-scale tree farms with no dwellings on site. And the house was serviceable for a transition house. All these aspects looked good, as far as Chance could see.

Whadya mean,"the house is serviceable?" The way you folks talk, there could be several other people involved, especially if this so-called Collapse comes down. Sounds like cramped quarters to me, Becky interjected.

Taken aback, *Well, that's a good point. I meant to say, the house is adequate shelter for several people under hardship conditions. Not great, far from ideal. But I want to remind folks that we are unlikely to find that hypothetical perfect place, especially in the talked-about time frame. Maybe we should compromise on the housing aspect if the rest of the package looks more desirable. Or, if you folks want, I can put this one on hold while we continue the search. How many have we checked out so far? Eight? Nine? I think I've seen seven of those and this one looks the best to me, all things considered. But by all means, check it out for yourselves.*

Becky had more to say but chose not to verbalize the communication, opting instead to gaze over the heads of the others, teeth clenched, one foot tapping the floor ¾ time. Waymer did want to see the land and would go the following day, alone or accompanied by anyone else who would like to come along. With her kid, Meadow, in school, Gaia asked to go along. As for Coho, it was clear he needed to powwow with Becky and hash it out. They'd all meet in a couple days, mid-afternoon at the local coffee roaster's, down the street.

Later that evening, however, Chance got a call from Coho. *Hey man, what's up?* An unexpected call from Coho meant something was going on.

Unnnnh! Some complicated shit is what's up. What are you doing tonight? Could we go somewheres where we could talk?

Chance readily gave up cleaning and reorganizing his apartment to meet his troubled partner. *Why not? How about Tiny's Tavern, over on Rumsfeld Ave? Gimme an hour. Oh, and I might bring along that guy I mentioned before. But I'll ask him to give us some privacy, if you want.*

Yeah, ok. See you there.

Over tall, cold pints of microbrew—for Chance and Blue—and coffee for Coho, the recover*ing*, never recover*ed*, alcoholic—the haggard, culturally-conflicted indigene laid out his predicament, a nasty gash conspicuous over his right eye. After introductions, brief small talk, Coho directed all of his attention to Chance.

Blue sat at the back of the booth, content to let these guys conduct their business. Chance said, *You had that looked at, man? Looks to me like it could take a couple, three stitches.*

Nah, it'll be alright. Long as I can learn to duck flying ashtrays, Coho responded sheepishly. Referring to his wife of eight years, *She's scared, man. She went along with the idea up to now thinking—hoping—I'd come to my senses. Her people were poor white trash; she grew up working in the fields, in the orchards. Washing clothes in the irrigation ditch. Always a race to the next job, the next payday. I think she hears about the countryside and she conjures up her childhood scratching, from one fieldworker's shanty to another, picking fruit, vegetables, any harvest still required to be picked by human hand, never getting ahead. She hated it, rightfully so, and never wants to go back to it. To her, giving up our shit-jobs and selling off our hard-won city assets, such as they are, in order to try and make it on the land is baa-ad* stretching it out, *crazy.*

With a deep sigh, looking off at nothing, Chance said, *Becky's scared. I'm scared. You're scared too, right? Hell, who wouldn't be? I mean, we're thinking about pooling our assets in a cooperative venture of significant real estate—pretty much on trust of each other. On faith that we can and will act for the good of the group, even when we annoy the shit out of each other personally. The difference is we're not packing Becky's baggage. And I seriously doubt if any amount of reasoning could lighten*

84

Becky's baggage.

I tried telling her it wasn't going to be like it was for her growing up, Coho said. *I don't think she believes me. I mean, she believes that I believe it. She just doesn't think we know what we're talking about. She <u>lived</u> it.*

Ok, so what do you want to do now?

I don't know. Me'un her, we been good for each other, especially since I got off the sauce. It ain't been no picnic; she's a hard woman when she gets her back up, this large, rangy man starting to blubber and tear up.

After an awkward minute, Chance reached over and rested his hand on the man's arm. *I don't want to be the cause of bad blood between you and your lady. Let's call it a night. We've got our meetup day after tomorrow; if you can make it, fine. If not, well, no hard feelings.*

* * * * *

Blue had sold his car to appease a few of his creditors and for a little spending cash, so Chance volunteered to help him out with some errand running around town. Without saying so, and despite lingering reservations, Blue was leaning towards throwing in with this group. They still seemed *like a gaggle of loonies,* he thought, but there was a passion and consistency to their lunacy that he found

85

appealing. Between stops at the laundromat, they picked up some sandwiches from a local deli and walked the couple blocks to the park by the river. It was chilly but they'd caught a break in the rain. It was in a lull of the topical conversation that he got Chance to elaborate more of the scheme.

If you don't mind, run some of that sustainability rap by me again.

Sure. In simple terms, a system is sustainable when energy input equals energy output. Now, as we know, that's never in perfect balance. And energy comes in different forms...

Like the sun's heat evaporating water only to precipitate it elsewhere; yeah, I got that part.

And plants converting sunlight into growth via photosynthesis. So that's two different energy cycles, right there.

Which carry on independent of human effect, right? Blue asked.

In the sense that they—and wind, and geothermal— were autonomous cycles millions of years before humans were around, and presumably will still be active after we flame out, then, yeah, they are independent of human effect. Except for climate change being demonstrably connected to greenhouse gasses discharged by Homo sapiens...

So what's the big whoop? I thought I remembered from high school physics something about energy not being created or destroyed; that it just changes form, is all.

The First Law of Thermodynamics: you got it! Well, the big whoop, as you put it, is that, thanks to humans' ability to find and process petroleum, thanks to petroleum-based agriculture—we're talking planting, fertilizing, harvesting, processing, and transporting to market, but especially synthetic fertilizers—the human population has more than tripled in the last century. A resource that took sunlight and plants and optimal geological conditions millions of years to produce is taking humanity two hundred years to exhaust. That's seriously out of equilibrium. And now that we are entering the twilight of the petroleum/natural gas economy, it's actually kind of scary because, in so many ways, there is no substitute poised to fill in. No techno-knight clad in glow-in-the-dark Kryptonite to gallop in and make it possible for us even to fertilize crops on anything like the scale we now manage without petroleum-based fertilizers, to say nothing about transporting goods—well, it just ain't gonna happen, Chance said, slipping between vernaculars effortlessly.

87

How the hell do you know? You could be pushing that notion to heighten the scare factor. That, or some other agenda, said Blue, waxing a little truculent.

I'm sorry. You're right, of course. I was taking liberties with semantics for emphasis: exaggeration, get thee behind me! Surely, nobody knows the future. However, given known technologies, and peer-reviewed hypotheses and analyses, there is no known replacement for petroleum, no "soft landing" out there.

So a "hard landing" means fundamental changes...

To strip away the platitudes and euphemisms, humanity, led by us Merkans, has been bingeing for a century, living well beyond our means, and a population crash is very probably in our collective future. Just because no media would touch this subject—too freaky to contemplate, and anti-Big-Business, besides—doesn't mean it can't or won't happen. Now, does it start in two weeks, or five years?

And while you're at it, how big a crash should we expect around here? asked Blue, starting to get into it. *There are bound to be regional variations...*

I don't think it's possible to know When, or How Big, in advance. But here's the thing: What kind of fool would you have to be to think this <u>couldn't</u> happen? So if you thought somesort of crash might happen, wouldn't it *be prudent to start making preparations? We're teetering out on the edge of an increasingly precarious, unsustainable lifestyle, willfully oblivious to the impending Deep Change about to be visited upon us—or more accurately, we'll visit upon ourselves.*

You know that postulation that energy can neither be created nor destroyed, only changed in form? Chance asked. *Well, there's nothing that says humanity needs to be a part of the equation. Personally, I wouldn't bet against Arthropoda, waiting in the wings—or is it on the wing?—for a shot as the next preeminent life form, but that's just me,* he said with a conspicuous shudder—from the wintry air or imagery of insects taking over the world, perhaps both.

A cast-off supermarket plastic bag hurried by touching the ground briefly before again being lofted in the chill breeze, a sail no longer tethered to its ship, pursuing some mystic destination down wind.

Ok. Count me in. I don't feel in my bones the immediacy or severity of the Crash like you do, but I can live with that if you can.

Yeah, that's ok; I've been living this riff for a couple of years now, forging it, tempering it, looking at it from different angles, trying to see from different eyes. I wouldn't expect you to see it like I do, reassured Chance.

The other thing is, I got nothing to lose. Plus, as you know, I basically got no assets to contribute.

I'm not too worried about your lack of material assets. And if you don't mind, let's pursue that "nothing left to lose" notion at another time. You'll be expected to bring a good work ethic, and be reasonably cooperative, hopefully easy going, as you seem to be. Other than that, hey, carry your own weight.

I gotta say, the job description on this one is pretty vague but I think you can count on me. Or I'll let you know when you can't, said Blue.

That's as much as anyone could ask, Chance replied.

* * * * *

At the coffee shop the next day, the first order of business was Waymer and Gaia's report of their impression of Loretta Hanson's farm. They both liked it but it didn't knock them off their feet. Pressed to explain, Gaia said, *I don't know what I expected, something esthetically grander, maybe. But I think it'll grow on me. In every practical detail, it seems like a reasonable choice, as I understand what we're looking for.*

I pretty much ditto Gaia, said Waymer. *It doesn't have a Yosemite backdrop, but everything seemed to check*

90

out. Nary a significant flaw, and I'm sure I'll live to regret that statement.

That afternoon's group comprised Chance; Blue; Gaia and her daughter, Meadow; and Waymer, all hunkered around two tables pushed together. Only two other patrons occupied a table on the opposite side of the room. While Gaia and Waymer were describing their take on the Hanson Place, Coho sidled in, no Becky in sight. By default, Chance chaired the meeting.

Less-than breathtaking in its landscapes, yeah, I know what you mean. But if that's its worst flaw, we'll be lucky, Chance said. *Are there any other general comments? Thoughts? Concerns? As we've said all along, this is a big, scary undertaking and we want to be sure we're making the right decision...*

If we agree to commit to this property, what's the immediate tab? asked Gaia.

As you know, the asking price of the house and outbuildings—such as they are—and acreage is $550K, said Chance. *Frankly, I'd like nothing better than to buy it outright. But we agreed to keep the 60:40 ratio. Whatever commitment we make toward acquisition of the land is to be accorded 60% weight of our total investment. The other 40% will provide resources for infrastructure, whatever is commonly held to enhance our dwellings, or other aspects* *of our lives beyond the land itself. The thinking was, we don't want to buy the most land we can possibly afford, and lack the resources to convert the place to a more comfortable, desirable, sustainable homestead.*

This is beginning to sound like real money, Blue said to an audience who knew he was bringing virtually no tangible assets to the table.

Indeed, it is. In most cases, it's all we got. So let's make it work for us. Who's for making this property the tie that binds us? Chance asked, rhetorically.

What say we take a break while we mull this over, proposed Waymer. In general assent, people got up to stretch, refill coffee cups, void their renal toxins, ogle the pastry cabinet one more time, and meet in pairs and small groups. Momentum was building. Guarded optimism was being expressed all around; a group identity was coalescing.

Chance brought the soaring *gemutlichkeit* back to a few remaining particulars, *You know, by talking to most folks before this formal event, I kinda knew where we stood, in terms of membership and funding. A few of us have had an informal discussion about inviting in another half dozen or so like-minded—and well-heeled!—people. Is there anyone who wants to speak in opposition to soliciting more members? As you do, please submit an alternative plan for additional funding.*

That last little hook caught at least two hypothetical opponents off guard. After a moment to collect her thoughts, Gaia, at first in halting speech, offered, *Well, I... I don't have a clear means of more money... But I think it's pretty clear we will pick up more members, if and when this seismic upheaval takes place. And we don't exactly know what we're doing going into it... So I guess I'm urging caution in packing on new members.*

Becoming over-populated is a legitimate concern, to be sure, responded Chance. *It's a big part of the human problem at the macro level, so let's take care not to let it become a problem at the micro level. Initial calculations, subject to renewed scrutiny and revision, suggest the Hanson place could support +/-30 people, assuming a successful harvest of 10 acres of grains and legumes, some source of carbohydrates that we can store. So there's that, on top of a shortfall of investment capital in relation to Santa's Wish List, said list advanced and approved by all.*

Perhaps if we had an explicit quota of people at, what, 200K a head?, threw in Waymer. *I don't mean to be crass, but let's spell it out.*

Actually, we were thinking of another six maximum, able to contribute at least 100K each, couples 150K, everybody carefully screened for needed skills and social compatibility, Chance said. *Do I hear a motion for a*

93

vote on this plan?

So moved, said Blue.

And seconded, added Coho. A show of hands indicated, in their quasi-Robert's Rules procedure, a unanimous decision to flush out another six or so scared folks with something like 600 thousand dollars. Easier said than done.

Or so one might think. At this point, Chance produced, as if by sleight of hand, a prototype public announcement and mission statement he'd been working on; he'd done some research and found out he could rent space at the local community college, as long as the purpose passed college-admin muster—non-profit promotion of a socially redeeming event; a seminar-like function at which the public might be informed or engaged on relevant issues. Or a reasonable restatement of the foregoing cluster of theme/methodology terms.

Take a look at these, Chance said, flashing mock ups of how they might appeal to people increasingly anxious about the looming change, curious about what hedges, what safeguards, there might be.

Stunned, several people got their first real experience at how many moves ahead Chance generally operated in this kinetic/never stationary, 4-D chess game of social pragmatics. Gaia, impressed with his thoroughness, said, *Pretty sure of yourself, aren't you? What if we'd voted the idea down?*

Chance shrugged, nonchalant; *I would've abandoned the idea,* he said, belying the belief he considered that a possible outcome. *Anyway, we did vote to increase membership, so this represents one idea on how to lure a few more potential members.* He left unspoken the understanding that she, or anyone else, was free to suggest other methods. None did.

March 15th was a little more than two weeks away.

<u>The come on</u> (to be posted around campus and advertised under *announcements/community events* in the local papers):

Interested in investing in something

that is ultimately *recession/inflation proof?*
(Of course you are! What fool isn't?)

Explore membership in a community
of like-minded individuals

Come to a *FREE* informational meeting

Saturday, March 15, 2:30 pm

at Cedar Creek Community College,
Trillium Hall 219

Refreshments served!

<u>The brochure</u> (handed out at the event):

*Who are we?

We're a group of folks who think the best hedge against an uncertain future—a possible seismic shift that could come about as a result of sudden economic, environmental, and/or social upheaval—such a hedge is *LAND.* That's right, land. But not just any land. A good part of it needs to be arable, and it needs to have year-round water. What else has value in this economy and is likely to have value in the next, no matter what form society takes? Actually, a lot of things, like tools, equipment and seeds; all have critical value *once we acquire the land.* If one were thinking of this as primarily a financial investment in the current economy, human-energy input in the direction of sustainable productivity should only enhance the overall value.

*What's to keep people from buying separate parcels?

People are, of course, free to invest as they choose. We emphasize pooling our resources in order to buy sufficient land to support a community committed to sustainable living as our stated goal out front. It looks to us that families, or small, disconnected groups, are likely to be too few in population to learn quickly enough and acquire enough skills to survive the most dire projections of social change. Well-disciplined groups in the 16-to-32-member range would seem to have the best chance of survival into, say, a third year by group-coordinated means. We fully intend to cooperate, share knowledge and experience with other communities, but that is a different issue for a later time.

*How is one's stake in this venture protected?

We are currently registering with the state as a non-profit, corporate partnership (LLC). The corporation, a legal entity, will own the land and other common assets; one owns shares in the corporation in proportion to the contribution, in the early phase. Said shares are transferable in the financial market. However, relative financial contribution, relative legal ownership confers no special exemption status in terms of fulfilling responsibilities, duties, and roles.

*How does this investment opportunity provide "job security?"

We are facing a serious financial crisis at present, along with worsening social conditions and increasing hardship—but not outright societal Collapse, may such an event bypass humanity, and certainly we Americans, altogether. Or not manifest itself for several years, though trends don't look good. Let's say, you put a chunk of your assets into the *River Rats* (our tentative name), but want to keep your job and a place in town. *If* the Collapse occurs sooner than expected, or if you were to lose your job, with no employment opportunities to replace it, assuming you could make it to the farm, you've got a home. A home that will require your full participation, along with everyone else's to sustain it, but one in which you will become an equal member. Your status or relative degree of power does not change, no matter how large the contribution; you may not buy a kingdom.

*What's the objective?

Our goal is to achieve a sustainable community within five years, not hesitating to use petroleum-powered devices, and any other high-tech means, to get us closer. Sustainability means, in general, the ability to live in approximate balance with the rest of the biosphere. It is subsistence farming. It is self-sufficiency. We hope to be able to literally live by our own careful management of the land. And hope we don't have to.

* * * * *

99

The Ides of March may have been sufficiently warm and dry to warrant cultivating the Roman countryside 2000 years ago; in the Pacific Northwest of the US, however, mid-March in an average year could be counted on to be cold, wet, and dreary, and this year was no exception. But the pale wash of fluorescence in the austere, utilitarian, internal, and thus, windowless room, along with its institutional central heating, belied the chill gray outdoors.

Some small-group conversations attempted to satisfy interpersonal curiosities while people filtered in. A couple of carafes of coffee, some paper cups and napkins, and a big platter of homemade cookies adorned a table near the door. A swarm of people hovered nearby, hitting the cookies like a school of barracuda on exposed flesh.

Despite the fact that "members" still outnumbered curious visitors, by a quarter to three Chance got things going with formal introductions, outlined their purpose, delicately referred to financial expectations of new members, and described the land the group had committed to. The audience was modest. Initially, six newcomers showed up—and two of those, a couple, disappeared during break.

Well into what had become the familiar pitch, a sales event in which the seller fully believed the product, Chance said, *It's an audacious thing we are proposing. I dare say, we all feel confident in our own abilities to contribute to the whole, but we are asked to believe that everyone else, a roomful of strangers, will make similar good-faith commitments.*

And ceding trust in our fellow human has not always been wise or justified, even under normal circumstances, Gaia interposed.

So this flies in the face of good judgment, in the conventional sense, Chance resumed. *But here's the deal: What choice have we got? If these projections play out, we're going to have to trust other folks. Better it be like-minded folks where we have the luxury of some time to grow together before the Collapse occurs. It sounds like I'm preying on your fears, but I think of it as an appeal to action, a commitment to a sustainable future, instead of floating along, waiting for your future to happen to you.*

I don't s'pose we want to get into parsing "the future that happens to us" vs. "the future we create" just now, interjected Ron, the mid-to-late-30s, academic over-achiever, and male counterpart of the couple. *But the choices we have are the very point. And so far, to my mind, you haven't made the case for such a devastating calamity.*

Utter silence while people considered the dialectic

required to fully engage Ron. An audible sigh, then Chance said, *Boy, you got me there. I made some inferences about people's background knowledge regarding a range of social arcs and trends. I assumed most of these folks would have already seen enough to be genuinely concerned for their children's future—to say nothing of their own. I figured we'd all be pretty much of the same orientation. You're welcome to stay, of course, but if you are not yet fairly convinced that global climate change is underway, along with an array of unknown consequences; if you don't think there is a convergence of increasing demand of petroleum and declining reserves, I can pretty much tell you would not be a good fit for this project...*

After a brief, whispered conference, the couple opted to remain. Again Ron spoke up, *If you're so sure this disaster is going to befall us all, why aren't you devoting your time and energy to raising public awareness?*

Good question, Chance said. *In terms of our goals, it's possible to see our fellow travelers as members of one of the following groups: 1) Deniers, affectionately called "Ostriches;" 2) Doubters, who recognize the possibility of a resource-supply collapse, and subsequent social meltdown; and 3) True Believers. The Deniers tend to be intractable optimists who refuse to believe our* government or our media would fail to alert or prepare us for such a threat. Also they can't accept that the magic combination of technology, imagination, and entrepreneurship would fail to save the day. Or the notion simply doesn't conform to their religious doctrines. Therefore, "it can not and will not happen."

The Doubters have several good reasons to be skeptical. First, these projections may be overly pessimistic: Look around; things aren't so bad. So what's the rush? Second, if these projections are true at all, this is going to be a profound social upheaval. No one would wish this on the human race; so, proceed with caution! Third, this seems like a huge risk; my fate is going to be tied to these or other folks in similar compacts. "Nothing in my experience has prepared me for this. Alarm bells are clanging!"

Doubters often harbor thoughts of a "Soft Landing." This view recognizes the likelihood of some profound changes in society, yet envisions a "readjustment" that we humans, and specifically, we Americans will accommodate—we always have!—with little or no loss of life. Still, many of these folks have seen and read enough to be genuinely alarmed. To those of you in this category, we hope to put some flesh on the body of this idea—put it in practical terms, provide a sense of how our plan might *be a wise alternative to taking your chances and doing nothing.*

Now for a little self-disclosure, or confession time, if you had somehow missed the cues up to now: I'm a True Believer. I cop to being a "Trubie" for the last couple of years. Probably, all True Believers start as Doubters; certainly I did. The more I read and the more I thought about it, the more convinced I became. And the surer I was about the need for translating thought into action. We Trubies tend to think there will be no soft landing, and wishing won't make it so. This has all the earmarks of a crash landing. Hence, the futility of sounding the alarm; no matter what we do, I think there's going to be a significant population drop off. We're not all going to make it. So my strategy has been to help organize and design a community, get it kick-started, before the social meltdown.

In which case, Blue plunged in, *it makes sense we get busy building bonds among ourselves while we build our subsistence homestead...*

After such a cognitively weighty interaction, Gaia suggested they take a break. No one opposed the idea. With visible relief, people bolted for the exit. Most people used the time to engage in small group discussions to get other people's take on points of concern. When they got back together, Ron and his unidentified female squeeze didn't return.

Resuming the dialogue, a young man who identified himself as Coyote, spoke up for the first time: *Who makes the day-to-day decisions on this collectively-owned land?*

We're committed to this being egalitarian. Everyone has a voice; each person has a say in decision-making, Chance said. *The actual process, in instances of disagreement, involves the tribal council, which hears all the commentary, and then tries to resolve the event. In rare instances when the council is unable to reach accord after due deliberation, it goes to the Elders for final judgment. But all this is a projection of a social experiment. It's important to stay flexible; perhaps try new approaches, as long as we all have equal authority in policy changes and group-level decisions, as long as strict equality is held to be our goal.*

Is there some religious affiliation involved? Coyote asked.

Gaia pounced without hesitation, *I'm happy to say there is not. You are, of course, welcome to bring whatever spiritual belief system you want, but you're going to have to keep it pretty much to yourself. No Sabbath, no time off to practice your own idiosyncratic rituals, and no proselytizing your fellow members. So I guess you can say we don't encourage it.*

The thing is, we're trying very hard to establish a group identity, Waymer ventured. *And while we don't want to squelch any individual identity, we hope to create a collective identity that is ultimately the more important.*

Coyote, expressionless, did not reveal any reaction to the commentary, merely nodding slightly.

Vic, an overweight software designer and computer techie, spoke up, *You know, I like what I've heard. A lot of the stuff the little lady and I've been kicking around, you folks have actually addressed—and give every indication of pursuing on a small scale. But I'd like to hear more about the organization's legal structure as it relates to the socio-political reality we got now. Bev and I were a little unclear on ownership-slash-investment rights as applies to today's laws of the land.* As DINKs, Vic and Bev had tucked away a tidy sum in just shy of a decade as professionals, ostensibly savings toward the purchase of a house.

Allow me to give a version, volunteered Waymer, who'd coaxed the couple into coming. *As I see it, we've got two obligations. One is to build confidence and trust among ourselves by operating as openly and clearly as possible. The other is to avoid taking short cuts with the rules and regulations in the society we find ourselves in today, thereby jeopardizing our whole effort. As long as this version of reality is subject to state and federal law, we intend to be law-abiding. We also have some ideas as to how we might organize ourselves, post-Collapse, but that's for a later discussion.*

Now, that sounds reasonable, but plenty vague—a little short of details, wouldn't you say? said Bev, Vic's considerably overweight wife. An energetic, ambitious middle school educator, Bev did not suffer fools lightly.

Quite eloquent, I thought, said Chance. *But to be specific, you will be issued shares of the corporation, registered with the state, according to assets contributed to the corporation. The corporation is the legal representation of the tribe; it owns the assets. It's all there in the brochure. You know, if you have legal doubts, we recommend you take any of the contractual stuff to your own lawyer before you sign anything.*

Waymer dove in, *Well, I'm about to sink two hundred K into this crazy scheme; you think I'm not scared? If you don't mind, I'd like you all to humor me with a little exercise; you can help me get over feeling scared. I have five words I'd like you to repeat with me.* Standing, walking around the room, *With a little practice, I want us to say them together and loud. The five words are: I. Will. Care. For. You.*

Most people went through the motions in their first attempt feeling foolish and self-conscious. The mutual display of outstretched arms, hands on each other's shoulders in this sophomorish exercise, like a giant football huddle, a "power circle," nothing more than a clever touchy-feely device. But little by little, entrenched doubts began to erode. In assuring all of these other people that you would care for them, you got, in return, each of them promising to care for you. By the third time, the assemblage full-throat shouted *I! WILL! CARE! FOR! YOU!* to startled passersby in the hallway, and there were no longer any holdouts. Six had become nine with the addition of Vic and Bev, and Coyote, and "The River Rats" bank account was pledged upwards of $400K, with more forthcoming.

Vic and Beverly's concerns had been answered. The words continued to satisfy as they pretty much always had. Now, it was more a matter for them to accede to the group and its spokesman, Chance, a level of trust gathered between and around the words.

They were off and running. At some point, they would have to close the "membership" to other investors; the very nature of sustainability/balance/homeostasis in a post-petroleum economy precluded it from being a come-one-come-all opportunity. But not just yet. They had less than ten committed members; they were still on the make.

A few more investors of significant means, if you please, to fatten up the coffers. The more money in the bank, the more investment in equipment and materials they could make in the current economy.

* * * * *

Go take a sister by the hand
Lead her far from this foreign land
Somewhere where we might laugh
again...
Horror grips us as we watch you die
All we can do is echo your anguished cry
And stare as all your human feelings die
We are leaving, you don't need us...

"Wooden Ships,"
Jefferson Airplane

The Hanson property transaction closed late-spring; in their final conversation Loretta Hanson inquired about the plans Chance had for the property, *if you don't mind my asking?*

Well, a small group of us are going to try to farm the place. I expect it will take us a while, but the hope is we'll be able to live off the land some day.

That's an admirable goal, to be sure. I wish you luck, said Mrs. Hanson, somewhat incredulous. Nothing in her life prepared her for self-sufficiency, a goal her grandparents' generation had begun to abandon with the proliferation of electricity and the gasoline engine, a goal her parents' generation had barely known.

By the way, if you were willing to part with your dog, I'd take him on and care for him, said Chance, sheepishly. *I'm probably out of line to even ask.*

No, not at all, she beamed. *How are you going to know unless you ask? As a matter of fact, I've been at wits' end trying to figure out a solution for Jack. I'm moving into a small apartment—I hope! Or, I'll alternate between my daughters and their families. As clever and mindful a dog as he is, it wouldn't work with him in either case.*

Oh, I'm so glad! I was impressed by Jack the first time we met. Can I compensate you somehow? Some money, perhaps?

Not on your life. As long as you treat him well, wagging a finger, adopting a mock-scolding manner.

I promise we'll take good care of him. And like now, he'll always have the run of the place, Chance reassured her. From the beginning, they agreed to have at least one person physically on site at all times. Coho and Blue would alternate at the outset.

Now was the time for the inevitably contested details to play out, especially as to how to allocate expenditures of something like 40% of the tribe's resources. Which projects to fund, which ones not? People were instantly thrust into participatory democracy, the negotiation of power. Every member was encouraged to walk through their common house and around the grounds, making notes as to how the place could be adapted to better suit their living there, keeping in mind the parameters inherent in self-sustainability, onerous though they may be in the current, profligate society. They were going to engineer a transition, or one would rain down upon them, and it would dictate the terms of survival such that most people wouldn't.

Where to locate next-generation energy-efficient housing for everyone, where/ how to position a windmill and photovoltaic (PV) arrays, and the limited electrification it would provide; it all needed careful consideration. One faction argued for patience investing in the high-tech realm. To these few, relatively near-term higher production efficiencies, tax incentives, and subsidies would make it economically worthwhile to wait. Assuming said glacial shift takes place before the Cataclysm, another faction was quick to counter.

After eight years of squandering the nation's social, moral, and economic capital, and furthering the assault on the biosphere—a latter-day *Dark Ages*—the country had elected a new administration from the opposing party and thus, had ventured tentatively into the politics of hope, as opposed to the previous administration's sustained campaign of fear. A shift in political will toward alternative energy sources seemed inevitable. Slowly, tentatively, alternative sources of energy were back to being supported as the most direct way to drastically reduce our outsized greenhouse gas contribution—to say nothing of the country's dependence on increasingly in-demand foreign oil.

In lieu of consensus on when and precisely what they were to invest in, the group decided to move ahead on the items of mutual agreement: they should fence a huge agricultural area, fence it soon while they could afford it, and use mechanized equipment to begin to cultivate it. Said fence should be a minimum of eight feet high to keep the deer at bay. They should secure water use rights to their little stream and build a small dam from which to draw water for household and irrigation use, though in the meantime they would continue to use well water via the electric pump, as long as they had commercial power.

Waymer had bought himself a seat at the table, particularly regarding financial matters owing to his largess, but truth to tell, any adult member showing an interest in the outcome of this or that event would be welcomed to sit in committee. Nobody had the moxie to come right out and pry Waymer's financial circumstances out of him. What was known: They were substantial, presumed to have come his way legitimately, by inheritance most likely. As we know, there's a lot of money out there, and thanks to Waymer, we know some of it is good money.

By the time the Crash had reached its apogee, Waymer would admit that his contribution to the tribe of, ultimately, half a million dollars, give or take, was the best investment he'd ever made. Whatever he kept in reserve from the tribe, to say nothing of most of the so-called wealth of the world's speculative free-market capitalism, would disappear within three short weeks, the following spring.

* * * * *

PART III

I pulled into Nazareth,
I was feelin' bout half-past dead;
I just need some place
where I can lay my head.
"Hey, mister,
can you tell me
where a man might find a bed?"
He just grinned and shook my hand;
"No" was all he said.
Take a load off Fanny;
take a load for free,
Take a load off Fanny
and you put the load right on me.

The Weight,
The Band

By the time Crow trudged back to Switzerland, the safe house, it was early evening. It had been drizzling for most of the walk back, and he was wet, as well as dog-tired. On the one hand, he was damn glad to get back this far with no major mishap; on the other, he could've let himself get talked out of going on alone without Paco, in the first place. Nobody would've said a thing; it'd been his choice. Thus, the +/-30-mile-roundtrip, hoofing it the whole way—that was his biggest mistake: he could've biked at least half way there and stashed it somewhere out of the way, and saved him walking half the distance. On the return phase packing, maybe, 40 lbs. of usable/tradable goods, he was unable to share the load with an absent partner. On no sleep, no real rest for 36 hours. All things being equal, his bike was still safely cloistered here for a ride over most of the final leg of the journey home. But that would be tomorrow.

Tonight, Crow was interested in hearing about the errant Paco—word had it that he'd come down with a fever and was resting under care back at the Haven—as well as any other scuttlebutt going on, but what *really* interested him was a hot cup of tea and a bite to eat, a place to sit near the wood stove so he could warm up and dry out, and soon curl up in an out-of-the-way place for some serious sleep.

Recently, in what people were beginning to call "Post-Crash," by sheer leap of faith Juan and Alyshka took on the role of hostellers, starting up this place specifically as a way station. They posted notices on all the known roads and trails within 4 or 5 miles of Switzerland—a curious name, given that neither Juan's nor Alyshka's roots were even close to geographic Helvetia. When everyone else was intent on constructing a defensive (if not belligerent) posture in relation to people outside their immediate group, these two brave souls *stuck it out there.* Middle aged, with no other family and little to lose, they thought to take a contrarian chance.

Their philosophy was absolute neutrality in all disputes. They acted on the principles of "live and let live" and "see, hear, speak no evil." They hoped people would see that they didn't pose a threat, they provided a service, and the service was of greater value than killing/robbing them of their meager goods. It was a bold experiment that had locals in this neck of the woods crossing their fingers, hopeful. The way it worked relied entirely on trusting the integrity and good will of their guests. If you had something, you shared.

Juan was a pretty handy woodsman, repairman, jack-of-all-trades; he kept a warm house (figuratively-and-literally) open to any peaceful person, any time. Alyshka

117

had already started a big garden, kept a tidy house, and was known to create amazing meals out of the likes of a handful of beans, a half-rotten onion, and some salt and spices. Nobody stopping for hospitality would neglect to share his/her extra food with them. It was what they served to the next set of passers by and how they themselves ate.

Already there were indications that Switzerland was being transformed into Message Central. Missed connections and communiqués going or coming, items and skills offered for sale or in urgent need, all posted in a sheltered part of the front porch. Could there be a Trading Post-slash-Inn far away?

Juan thought that networking—once people relearned that strangers are mostly trustworthy, that trust is expedient, born of mutual need—would make them individually and collectively more resilient, adaptable, and would enrich them socially. All would agree, predicated on cooperative values as the basis for transactions.

Potentially problematic, however, were the remaining stockpiles of gasoline that they all knew were out there. Presumably, most were in depots under the control of military establishments around the world. But some, here and there, were horded by pockets of neo-feudal lords, the hold-over or the newly self-appointed aristocracy, defended by their mercenary armies, having bought a degree of continued power and mobility. Alas, such people did not operate on anything like a collectivist, egalitarian paradigm. Convoys of such people, spectral *Mad Max* phantasmagoria, were said to have visited havoc on distant communities too near state and county roads. Since no one in the tribe's experience had direct knowledge of such acts, it was hard to know what was fear mongering and what was a realistic threat.

Crow awoke stiff and surprised to find he'd slept through the night without interruption. Having devoured the serving Alyshka had put together the evening before—a thin but tasty vegetable soup, a rough cornbread muffin, and a big mug of mint tea—he was good for about 15 minutes, sitting next to the wood stove, steaming like wet laundry, contributing less to the conversation with each passing minute. Juan recited their events since he was there just the evening before, while Alyshka cleaned up the kitchen. A few people had passed through during the day, mostly newcomer locals curious about the Switzerland potential. They had no other overnight guests, with none expected. By this time, he could hardly keep his eyes open; Juan showed him an upstairs room with a clean mattress, pillow, and some blankets. He was out within three minutes.

In the dawn, he folded the blankets and stacked

them with the pillow on top before going downstairs. Juan was stoking the stove, getting it to roar; Alyshka was uttering incantations—or maybe it was a simple children's song in an unfamiliar language—while mixing flours of unknown origin, a leavening agent, some water and dried fruit into a batter, destined to become a whole-pan pancake.

Juan set a steaming mug of the ubiquitous mint tea in front of him as he sat down. After pleasantries, Crow said, *You know I didn't find any food, right? If I did, you'd be the first folks I'd share it with.*

Yeah, we figured as much, Juan said. *Don't worry about it.*

The next time a River Rat passes by Switzerland, I'll see to it some edibles come your way. You folks are doing a great thing here. We all want to keep this a going operation, Crow said, wanting to believe the "all" part more than he did.

Could you use some sheets? I think I found about four new twin sets. Also, I could let you have some of the eating utensils, if you want 'em.

Why, thank you, Crow, Alyshka answered. *That's very kind of you; we're pretty much set as to cooking and eating gear. I'd given some thought to accumulating more sheets for guests—we've got our own, mind you—but I'm*

120

not too partial to washing 'em, and I'm pretty sure Juanito feels the same, glancing over at her partner, head bowed, nodding slightly.

Crow stretched out the visit another hour or so, enjoying the comfort and leisure the couple's warm hospitality afforded before gathering together his dried garments and backpack, and taking leave. This last leg of the journey back to the turf was over rougher terrain, as the course took him farther from the shell of the city. Rougher in several places where he'd have to walk his bike, but increasingly more familiar. And safer. There weren't a lot of people 25, 35 miles out from the urban remnants, and the ones even farther out were hunkered down, lying low, having survived the Fall, believing their best chance of survival was to stay below the radar of societies of any stripe. For now, anyway. Most of the folks nearer in were carving out a niche in this vicinity and were mutually known or known about: Someone in that tribe had had some interaction with someone from another group, who knew people in your tribe. It might be a tenuous relationship, but essentially no resident of these parts wanted to provoke hostilities.

As he drew closer, within a couple miles or so of the homeland, he thought he saw movement along the trail some 200 yards ahead. It was getting on to late afternoon

121

and he'd been lucky with the weather for a change; he'd caught a few light showers but was in the midst of a prolonged respite. The area was wooded hills and he was about to drop into the watershed where the family turf lay. He quickly dismounted his bike and hunkered down; sure enough, two people were taking their time, animated by some consideration, heading his way. He was pretty sure they were his people but he squatted down beside the trail, inconspicuous, until they were within 50 to 60 feet and he could make them out: It was Coho and Flora, and good timing, too. He hailed them so as not to startle them. They were delighted to come across him, just not as delighted as he was. They were on patrol, looking out for anything unusual, and, since he was expected back, keeping an eye out for him.

On the way back, Flora and Coho took turns shouldering the backpack as they exchanged updates. Paco's condition seemed unchanged, stabilized—no one else reported symptoms. Otherwise, things were running on a predictable course with the tribe. The day before, two of their hunters had staked out the block of salt left in a small clearing some distance east of the farm and shot with crossbows a probable two-point buck, antler buds just erupting. It'd taken them until late to clean the kill, haul it back to the house, skin it, and hang it in a high, dry location, even after recruiting more help. Tonight there'd be venison liver, heart, and backstrap for dinner! To go with whatever miserable, tortured cornmeal concoction the cooks came up with.

Crow was beginning a rough account of his discoveries, his run in with the Rolling Stones members, and the dramatic changes taking place at Switzerland, when they arrived. What a relief! A shower and a change of clothes after a warm meal with the family were going to be appreciated the more for having forfeited the experience the two previous evenings.

Shoes off, seated, feet up, some chamomile tea in hand, Crow described his solo foray chronologically to several family members, assembled for a casual social hour before dinner, a labor pool should the kitchen staff, in full-throttle dinner preparation, need a task performed; otherwise, they were free to amuse themselves as long as they stayed out of the way of those on task. As people unloaded and spread out the bounty from his trip, Crow explained why he chose the accumulated goods, where he had come by them, and he described his encounter with the dead woman. He then gave a detailed accounting of meeting Deke and No-Name of the Rolling Stones.

Were you scared? asked Blue.

Damn straight, I was, Crow responded. *Especially*

of that weaselly kid who kept edging up on my flank and wouldn't display any human emotion. I couldn't read 'im at all.

Likely, traumatized by events during the Crash, offered Waymer.

You did exactly right, Chance said; *surrendering the shovel got you out of that pickle, no doubt.* Other Council members on hand praised him for the garden seeds, bicycle tire tubes, and especially, the canning jar lids. Gaia was effusive in her praise about the large cooking pot, and everyone was grateful for the additional sheets and blankets. By this time, the aroma of meat cooking, a fairly rare occurrence anymore, was rippling through the group.

Fortunately, they didn't have to wait long; Amanita signaled Tad to call folks from the dorms and bade the rest of them wash up for dinner. The kitchen staff doled out a slightly larger portion to Crow without fanfare, knowing he was ravenous. He nodded in appreciation. There wasn't a lot to go around but the few mouthfuls of thin-sliced backstrap, as well as a portion of the quick-fried liver were sheer ambrosia. The heart had been stuffed with rice and spices and baked; it too, was marvelous. Less so, the old cornbread standby. Chewed slowly, it filled up one's stomach and rounded out the meal. The following night there would be an herb seasoned, slow-cooked roast, a real treat of which this was a mere prelude.

Over dinner Crow elaborated some of his impressions of Switzerland. *Personally, I think they're fulfilling a great role. I mean, we hope to mature into a regional network, don't we?* Murmurs of assent all around. *Well, it's pretty clear this local version of a communication and trade hub is a bare-bones, skin-of-your-teeth operation. They're going to need a lot more help if they're going to make it.*

Glancing at Coho and Gaia, Waymer said, *Why don't we take inventory of our food stores tomorrow towards sending some grains down to Switzerland?*

Right. I'm on it. But it's tricky business trying to estimate how many bodies we can feed, times how many days, Gaia said.

Especially with our summertime gardening successes a big question mark, Coho chimed in. *Right now, we're stretched pretty thin. I think we ought to hold a council meet and hash this out.*

I agree; let's have a council tomorrow night, said Amanita from the kitchen, starting cleanup with two of the juvies. *If we think we've got enough, we could send something the day after tomorrow.*

* * * * *

Crow knew before starting out on his sojourn that he would be back in the conjugal loop the evening of his return, if he so chose. Usually, opting out of one's turn meant s/he sacrificed the first of the three days allotted in the sequence. In his case, he would've been permitted postponing his round of *midnight sowing*, owing to having just returned from a three-day/two-night, +/- 60-mile trek. However, having first confirmed Sparrow was available that night, Crow was attuned to a little *skinship*, some physical warmth and sensuality.

He wasn't going to mind how it came out. In either case, Sparrow hopefully would be compliant: hot, wild, sticky, sweaty sex; inandout, upanddown, overandunder, foreandaft; an hour replete with unrestrained passion—*Not in your most depraved dreams*, he muttered to himself. More likely, a few minutes of gentle fondling, caressing, to remind the fingertips how and where things are, to relearn peaks and valleys, fields and forests, perimeters and parameters; the electricity generated when lips encountered other familiar and missed lips (though they be low-voltage sparks this night), then a quick descent into the dark abyss; a deep, dreamless unconsciousness. *Now you're talking reality.*

Most folks got a shower every other day; after three

days' absence, in the same clothes, Crow qualified for the front of the line. Wearing thin, though it was not late, he nodded to Sparrow his readiness for a shower when she was.

After gauging his fatigue, Sparrow observed, *The Blackbird's fixin' to get all hot and wet. Then,* to the amorphous second person plural, *we bid you goodnight.*

Of necessity, showering was perfunctory; water itself wasn't scarce, it was *hot* water that was limited, and took most of the day to accumulate enough to bathe 8 or 10 bodies. He and Sparrow took robes and headed for the sheltered alcove on the side of the house where the steaming, elevated tank stood. Partly exposed to the elements, in the dead of winter, for example, a 3-minute shower—couples were allotted 5 minutes—took grace and careful coordination, a trade off between the need to get clean and enduring the biting cold in the process; however, this spring-like April was noticeably warmer than in the throes of winter.

Crow enjoyed upwards of a minute of tingling hot water before stepping out of the direct spray. He then lathered himself from head to toe while Sparrow showered. Then quickly, the roles reversed for his rinse, then hers. A final 30 seconds of shared spray took place, bodies fused, accompanied by considerable good-natured squeezing, poking, tickling, and groping. A quick, mutual towel off and off to their boudoir, as Crow referred to it. Sparrow had prepared the bed beforehand.

Pressed together for the few minutes it took to warm up the bedding, he enjoyed a kind of romantic play, indulging a mock-lover's dialogue, *Do you still love me?*

Not to be out-maneuvered, especially since this was a familiar routine, she was up for the game, *You know I do, lover.*

I'll bet you say that to all the guys.

To which she offered a variety of cagey responses, according to the circumstances. Tonight, *No, not to all of 'em.*

Suggesting to Crow, *only the ones who'd asked her,* as he had. For Sparrow, stringing him along was part of the game; keeping it just a little ambiguous made it all the more exciting.

About the time they'd managed to warm up the bedding enveloping them, conversation trailing off, he brushed his lips ever so lightly over hers, a brief flutter of butterfly wings. No noticeable reaction.

So I do it again but slower over those slightly quivering, slightly pursed lips. And again, this time my lower lip gently between hers. Then, there's no more she-and-I, just some psychic/physiological entity somewhere

between and around and through Sparrow- and-Crow for
some uncountable minutes.

Meanwhile, the miracle of the extending male appendage had been occurring, firm and slightly pulsating, unable to be ignored. Two strong, diametrically opposing urges propelled him now, one hormonally driven: the beautiful serpent, Eros, had arisen. He well knew it could be a transcendent experience, to be truly in thrall of the serpent. Which, of course, would have been his unequivocal choice under normal wear and tear, but he was obliged to acknowledge the other compelling urge: surrender to gravity, submit to entropy, both of which were implacable and would win in the end. Sparrow was reaching for a condom on the nightstand when he stopped her. *It's such a turn on that you like kissing as much as me,* he whispered, as non sequitur.

Yeah, me too, she answered, thinking talking about it wasn't going to make it better, hoping for more without saying it.

Another kiss of fading passion from Crow, by way of a promissory note, a rain check for something more substantive, redeemable at a future date, and while she gave that a moment's consideration, he fell fully asleep.

Note to self, she thought: *Remind me to school this guy that it's bad manners to build expectations you have no intention of fulfilling.* Not that this was unpleasant, him cradled in her arms, oblivious, safe. *All right, maybe his intentions didn't have much to do with it,* she conceded, after she'd come down a little and her pulse had returned to normal.

* * * * *

Some hours later, Sparrow awoke to very faint, gentle tapping at the door and someone calling her in a low voice. It was Blue. Agitated, he wanted her to come with him to the other private room upstairs, requisitioned from love-nest status as temporary sickbay. Paco's condition had worsened; Gaia had been summoned. They didn't know what else to do. Getting up, dressing quickly, she barely roused Crow who was mollified, to the extent he was conscious enough to care, that she would be back soon.

Two kerosene lamps illuminated the room, one on the chest of drawers opposite the door and one on the nightstand next to the bed where Paco lay covered to his chest in a sheet, drenched in sweat, delirious. Several layers of blankets were bunched at the side of the bed for the phase of his illness when he was profoundly chilled. Gaia and Amanita had taken his temperature a half hour ago; *took it twice cause they didn't believe they'd gotten it right the first time,* Blue said. It was just under 105 degrees—the temperature at which adult brain cells begin to melt like butter. They'd done what they could to get the kid to drink some water, not very successfully, Blue thought. Gaia had gone to retrieve anything useful from their medicine stash.

We got to try to break that fever, Sparrow said, looking at Amanita questioningly.

I've been dabbing his face with cool water every few minutes, was Amanita's response.

Sparrow drew some fresh water in a stainless basin and dipped washcloths in it. These she applied to the wild-eyed, fitful young man starting with his face, alternating cloths re-rinsed in the basin. By the time she'd gotten to wiping down his arms, he had stopped being delirious and submitted peacefully to his sponge bath. *Help me hold him up and let's see if we can get some of this rose hips and chamomile tea down him.* Barely conscious and very weak, he would only take the liquid by tablespoon, a slow process.

Gaia hurried in; she'd spent some time going over their meager medicine supply. She found two types of antibiotics, both out of date, which she'd brought anyway. Except for aspirin, nothing else looked like it might apply in Paco's case. While Amanita checked out the antibiotics in their PDR copy in the light of the second lamp, the others reviewed what they knew in worried tones. *He's got*

131

somesort of raging infection, right? Sparrow queried.

Yes, but is it viral or bacterial? Gaia countered. *What other symptoms does he have?*

Blue spoke up: *I checked him over pretty carefully late afternoon; I couldn't find any external problems. He was listless, with no specific pain, just achy muscles consistent with a fever. Unresponsive. His temp at that time was around 101F.*

So if we shoot 'im up with antibiotics and it's a viral infection, it probably wouldn't hurt 'im. Just not do 'im any good, is all, Sparrow offered, hopefully.

Frustration apparent in Gaia's voice, *But another issue is, assuming it's bacterial, will our antibiotics be appropriate for the infection? Or enough to kill it off, as opposed to knocking it down only to have it come roaring back in a more virulent form?*

Amanita reported that one of their antibiotics was targeted for mucous membrane infections, like eye or mouth infections, and not indicated for general internal purposes. The other one had more systemic application but the regimen called for a whole week of hefty doses—a condition they were not supplied to meet—and should be accompanied initially by an additional medicine they lacked.

Paco's shallow breathing punctuated the silence as

the knowledge settled in that they didn't have enough information, and probably didn't have the correct range of antibiotics, to medicate him further. In all, they'd been able to get most of a cup of the herbal tea into the limp body. Finishing the body wipe down, Blue noted a faint rash appearing on Paco's neck and chest. *What do you think is going on here?* he asked no one in particular.

Examining the area in question, Gaia said, *let's hope it's just a reaction to his fever. Because, if memory serves, that's also a symptom of meningitis.*

At least he's resting peacefully now, offered Amanita. *Blue and I've attended him for quite a stretch now; what say we go get some sleep?* Blue giving every semiotic indication of affirmation.

That's a good suggestion. Sparrow?, said Gaia, glancing at her for confirmation; she nodding, *Sparrow and I'll stand watch.*

Encouraging the decision, *Sure; we'll come get you if there's any change, or if we need you.*

Be sure to do a thorough wash up; we don't know whether this condition is contagious or not, Gaia said as a final comment.

They brought up on either side of the bed the chairs Amanita and Blue had used during their vigil. *He was here when I came late last July. How'd you come to meet him?*

133

Sparrow asked.

He just showed up one day hanging around the area; people would catch sight of him before he'd disappear into the underbrush. 'Bout the 3rd or 4th time we'd spotted him, we started worrying that he was spying on us; you know, gathering information for another tribe to raid us, or something. So we doubled up patrols and checked farther out, but nobody could find any sign of other people in the nearby area—except for feral boy, here.

How'd you get him to come in?

At first we weren't trying to scare him off, but we weren't especially encouraging, either. Then, over days, when we felt more confident he wasn't involved in some malign agenda—and we could see he was becoming less-hinged by the day, starving right in front of us—we started leaving food out where he could find it, like you might for a damn raccoon.

So he could see you didn't mean him any harm.

Yeah, except he was a little slow figuring it out. Or was exceptionally wary; either way, several times he missed the food to other critters beating 'im to it. We finally flagged a lidded box that had a hasp on it so coons, packrats, and other critters couldn't get into it; he figured it out quick enough. Before long, we'd moved the box out in the open, chained it to a long spike we drove deep in the ground so he couldn't drag it off in the bushes, and made him come get the food in broad daylight. Hell, even Jack got used to him, stopped barking at 'im. He'd show up looking sheepish and we'd smile and wave. "Hey! What's your name?" Like that.

That's amazing. I had no idea.

He couldn't've been with us more than a month before you found us. The most profound transformation I'd ever witnessed. From minimally verbal, barely social to, well, what'd you think of him at first?

You know, I didn't think much about him at all. Most folks communicate important information via language, wouldn't you say? Sure enough, when I got here, several people were not shy about approaching me, primarily via that medium, while Sr. Paco was more on the quiet side. He did talk when he had a stake in the outcome of the subject, but even then, he didn't waste words.

Otherwise, he'd just ignore you. Eccentric, I thought, but not necessarily bad-eccentric.

On the theory that eccentricities of the old order, on balance, are more an asset than a liability, in post-Apocalyptic times?... Yeah, I'm down with that. But Paquito, here's, eccentricities were only compounded and made worse by the Collapse. His deep past is still mostly a *mystery but his immediate past—say, in the lead up before we took 'im in—had to've been pretty wretched. With us, at least he ate, slept, bathed, and interacted with people— even if on a limited basis. Did you know he's bilingual?*

I did know that; I think there's a slight accent. His parents were illegals who came here without any English, but he was born here, Sparrow stated. After a pause, *It's funny to refer to "here" from the old paradigm,* she continued, pensively. *The here has changed big-time; we no longer think it necessary to identify what obsolete nation-state you were born in. Boy, do old habits die hard.*

Amen to that, Gaia added.

As neither woman had an anecdote to add, the conversation trailed off. With Paco's rhythmic breathing, they soon lapsed into a shallow, restless sleep, themselves.

Then, something. Sparrow couldn't say what, but something awakened her—an unfamiliar sound? Her stiff neck, from having dozed, head slumped on shoulder? Whatever the reason, she couldn't have slept long. Looking up she took in Paco's utterly still form, as if asleep but no longer breathing. She looked at Gaia, in as equally uncomfortable a position as she herself had just been, sound asleep, then back to the dead boy/man, *former* family member, *former* lover, *former* partner on many a task. Drained of emotion, she thought what it meant for him to die/be dead, and what it would mean for her to die.

After awhile, she got tired of thinking altogether and got up and shook Gaia, who sat bolt erect and slowly took in the surroundings. *He's gone,* Sparrow said. *Must've been just a few minutes ago.*

Gaia checked for pulse in a carotid and finding none, nodded to Sparrow before pulling the sheet up over his head. *There's nothing to do now; we've got maybe three hours before daylight, if we're lucky. Might as well get a little sleep; what d'ya say?*

You talked me into it, said Sparrow, stretching. *Do you think I should tell 'Nita n' Blue? Because I said I would.*

Shit, I don't know; I don't think it'll matter. Watching Sparrow heading for the door, *Then again, it sure as hell could. If it was me, 'stead of them, I'd want to be told. Even out of a sound sleep. Though I'm not sure I could tell you why.*

Yeah, I see what you mean. They deserve to know sooner than later, having nursed 'im much of the day. Even if the timing might not be that important to them, it's not for us to second-guess. Ok, see you all too soon.

Sparrow scrubbed her hands, then arms, then face and neck in the tepid water, warmed since people had gone to bed. After, she went out to the women's sleeping

137

quarters. *Amanita,* shaking her shoulder. *Amanita! It's me, Sparrow. Sorry to wake you but I wanted you to know that we lost 'im. Just a short time ago. We did what we could.* Strong hug from Amanita, and a loud sob. *Poor Paco.* Triggering her own tears, then crying/laughing mixed together. *Did I do the right thing waking you? Nothing's happening at least till morning.*

Yes, you absolutely did the right thing.

Good, because I gotta go let Blue know next. Be thinking what we should do to celebrate Paco.

At the men's dormitory she had to walk carefully among the shoes and clothes at the end of many beds, five out of a possible eight beds occupied tonight. Finally she located Blue and nudged his foot. He groaned, so she nudged it again. *Hunh? Who is it?*

It's me, Blue. It's Sparrow. He's gone. There was nothing more we could do. I just wanted to let you know. Sorry to wake you.

Sitting up, *No, that's alright. I'm glad you told me.* A hug here, too. A physical bond to compensate for the ineffectual words in establishing a shared sorrow.

She paused to see if Blue had anything else to say and when he didn't, she said, *I gotta go; if you can think of anything that might be a good Paquito sendoff, well, let's talk in the morning.*

138

Crow had not moved in the two, two and a half hours since she'd left. Whatever he'd been dreaming was gone in the first minute of Sparrow's return. Her cool body slipping into bed was a delicious sensation, just barely touching in a few discrete points of contact. It woke him immediately. Kissing her face—slowly approaching her mouth—he tasted the dried salt-stains of former tears on a cheek. He found the other cheek to confirm and whispered, *Are you alright?*

She slowly nods her head. He feels the motion more than sees. No words are requisite, none forthcoming. At first, she's just barely willing to return the kisses. And then she is greedy. Languid fatigue evaporates, displaced by a new imperative. This time he is ready for the formality of protection. Sparrow rolling it over him is tactilely, sensuously exquisite. Time to lose selves in sheer animal pleasure.

* * * * *

In the morning, over tea and the breakfast biscuit, the ad hoc funeral committee talked over possible variations to Paco's send-off ceremony. Chance's advocacy for burial was mostly a formality. By the time they got together, they'd pretty much dispensed with the notion of cremation; even in prime timber-growing country, it is hard to justify the use of so much wood in this way. *I guess you all remember we've got Vic and Beverly planted up the slope behind the house.*

Pointing in the general direction, *Off East at the tree line? Yeah, that's a good place,* Coho said to general assent. *Well, if we all agree on this method and location?...* Chance affirmed and asked at the same time. *We'll need a couple of people to take care of the dig.*

I'm on it, Waymer responded. *I'll recruit a couple of the juvies and maybe whoever's on the labor pool could relieve us in an hour.*

We'll see to it that happens, Chance reinforced. *Choose a good spot, will yuz? Paco seemed to like panoramic views; more than once, I'd catch him gazing off at the surrounding landscape with that wistful smile you'd sometimes see on 'im.*

Gaia asked Tooloose and Owl, Paco's nearest in age and closest buddies, to be in the group to organize the funeral ceremony. Maybe they needed another member to be in the ad hoc group; what did they think? Who would they recommend to join them?

Owl and Tooloose had a brief, semi-private conference before Tooloose offered, *Maybe we should open it up to anyone who wants to participate.*

Good idea. In terms of decision-making, there's

140

something to be said for small in population but what the hey. Everybody had a stake in Paco's life; they should all have a say on how we send him off.

Ok, we'll spread the word. What's our time-frame, asked Owl?

Important issue! In the old days—a couple'a years ago, and for a long time before—I think an unembalmed body was legally required to be in the ground 24 hours after death, to minimize the smell accompanying decomposition. But that would put the limit at around three o'clock tomorrow morning. The weather's still pretty cool so I think we can push that clock back seven, eight hours.

So a ceremony tomorrow, say, mid-morning, affirmed Tooloose.

Owl completed the thought, *which gives us time to get the message out for an after-dinner meet, and for everyone to be giving thought to how s/he might participate or contribute to the event.*

You've stolen the words from my mouth! That was breathtaking in its clarity, said Gaia, unable to resist dishing some irony to go with the compliment.

Also, let's ask the people we talk to to pass the word themselves.

That evening, around their communal meal, the

141

great luxury of roast venison haunch and home-made noodles, this exquisite meal was rather eclipsed by the impatience to get on with the Council Meeting *after* the dinner. Rules were rules and heated discussions were not to be tolerated during the meals.

The sole reason for this meeting of course was as a forum for people to offer perspectives on how they should take leave of Paco. Waymer and Coho confirmed that the burial site was ready. Blue suggested, *Paco's our first loss since we've all been together as a family. I think everybody should be heard on this. You young'uns got anything to say?*

Diana said she'd like for everyone to hold hands and quietly think about Paco. Gaia said, *I agree, Diana, and I think we all agree. Will you take the leadership on this event? When you think the time is right, call us to hold hands in a Paco bond?*

With a little coaxing, she was fine with the idea. Meadow had helped Amanita wash and wrap Paco's body that morning and was still teary eyed. *You know, he was partial to that ol' hippie song, "Joy to the World." Maybe we could all sing it together, to show our connection to Paco,* she said.

Many praised the idea, Crow admitting he didn't know the lyrics. *Just the first verse, is all I remember,*

Meadow said. *I think this is how it went:*

Jeremiah was a bullfrog (in a high, pure voice)*; was a good friend of mine.*

Never understood a single word he said, but I sure liked to drink his wine,

And he always had some mighty fine wine.

Singing, Joy to the world, all the boys and girls,

Joy to the fishes in the deep blue sea, and joy to you and me. Smiles and nods of approval.

Shy when group attention came to him, Tad had nothing particular to offer. Several others said they wanted to say something about Paco to the group, read a poem or a prepared statement, and everyone agreed this should happen in no particular order. Coyote hung back, withholding public comment, as was his pattern. Chance complimented the suggestions and the unforced, unregimented way this memorial event was coming together: *It seems to me that this is an expression of us as a family—maybe as formal an expression as we are going to get—and a way to help unify us. Maybe this is the right time to review who we are.*

That's got me all over it, said Sparrow. *For example, who are we in terms of our name? A lot of identity is tied up in a name. Personally, I've never been that charmed by being a River Rat. What's that make this place, our Rat*

Hole?

Good point. Whadja have in mind as an alternative? queried Waymer.

Well, I was flipping through a local writer's novel and she was talking about the origins of the word Pagan. *It's Latin, of course; comes from* Pagus, *the word for* farm. *Turns out, once Rome got established, even then, there was this tendency where the urban dwellers considered themselves the cutting edge of knowledge, fashion, the arts, what have you. So their country cousins, those hicks 'n' crackers, the farm-dwelling Pagans, were the simple folks who followed the old customs and believed in the old, traditional deities.*

Interesting, Chance responded. *Personally, I'd rather we not try to resurrect Jupiter, Neptune, Minerva, Apollo, Venus, or the rest of the Roman pantheon, as our gods. But maybe we could venerate something like the Spirit that Inhabits All Life, without having to be specific. And still be Pagan, that is.*

Sure, Blue interjected. *We could be Pagans and leave it up to the individual to interpret for him/herself what "it all means,"* making the quotation-mark gesture with the first two fingers of both hands. *Because, like Chance, I'm against codifying rituals. No dogma, if you please!*

Yeah, I like it, Amanita chimed in. *How about some more input, though; anybody else got some ideas? Happy with being a River Rat? Willing to become a Pagan, instead? Or do you have another suggestion?*

To tell the truth, I gave some consideration to our place being called Dirt, a sheepish Coho chimed in. *Half the year we could be Mud. We'd be Dirt Farmers, I suppose, though I'd much rather be a Dirter, or a Dirtie. What do we do? We work the dirt. Where do we live? We live on dirt, in dirt, with dirt, at Dirt. On the one hand, there's definitely something humbling and ennobling about all-too-literally living on the land. But I can see how that other, ironic sense may not work for everybody.*

Actually, I'm instantly attracted to that ironic element, Crow responded. *But for the sake of advancing preparation of Paco's send off, what say we adopt Pagans as who we are formally, this place as our Haven—and try on Dirt informally? Nobody's saying we can't change all this again, if we want, down the road.*

Sure, I'll go for that, Coho said. *I proposed Dirt mostly for the humor in it.*

Anybody else got a dog in this race? asked Gaia, scanning the room. *Any more farfetched suggestions?*

There was a minute or two while the assemblage looked around and took stock of each other, and in so doing, took stock of themselves. Finally, Amanita said, *Let's take a vote and see where we stand?* In the end, it was unanimous for the change.

Well, good for us, said Chance. *I think we're pretty well set; let's plan on this ceremony from ten, tomorrow morning. Please be preparing what you're going to read or say. After everyone has a chance to say something, I guess I'll lead us in a closing shout, a group hug, and we'll bury him. And that'll be it.* Since there was no further comment on the subject, the council adjourned. Many turned to other tasks, some with private thoughts on becoming a Pagan, an event predicated on the loss of one of their own.

Family members began heading up the hill from about 9:30, some in what passed for finery, others in plain clothes. Earlier, Paco's body had been brought up to the burial site on a litter by two teams of four. The body had been completely wrapped in a sheet, except for the face. It was understood that two designates from each team would be called on to wrap the face, then muscle the body into the hole in as dignified a process as they could muster. Shovels would then be handed around for all to take a turn.

In that big voice Chance could muster, he drew the attention of the group. *We are gathered here today to take leave of Paco, our beloved family member...* Gaia had alerted Diana to call the group early in the ceremony. *Would anyone like to say something at this time?*

On cue, in her clear, strong, high-pitched voice, Diana said, *Could we all please form a circle of hands for a minute of silence? I think of it as our private hopes and prayers, but you can think of it any way you want.* With clasped hands, some heads bowed, all waited for Diana to be the first to relax her grip. It was a long couple of minutes.

What the create-as-you-go ceremony lacked in professionalism was more than compensated for by the personal and heartfelt outpouring of unity in grief. Tears flowed freely at many of the comments and in particular, Meadow's leading the group in *Joy to the World.*

Coyote surprised everyone at a pause, by saying in a loud, ragged voice, *Adios, Paco!* When no more thoughts were forthcoming, Chance asked the family to shout after him, as loud as they could: *Thank you, Paco!*

A reasonably committed response, *Thank you, Paco!*

One more time, THANK YOU, PACO! This time, they could hear the echo, *'nKYU Pa Co.* A few seconds of silence, then from Chance, *Pagans forever!*

PAGANS FOREVER! came the thunderous response, accompanied in equal parts, by smiles and tears.

The ground was wet and so getting the body into the

hole neatly was going to be awkward. Tooloose was on one side of the upper-torso rope when the corpse folded at the hips and wouldn't lie flat without a little help. Cursing under his breath, Tooloose lay down on the tarp beside the grave, the better to reach the hung-up body. Straining, he let out a *Whoop!*, and fell on top of the corpse, thereby rectifying the problem. He soon appeared with a sheepish grin, quite muddy and a little spooked, before hands were offered and he could clamber out, to the unconcealed merriment of everyone.

Those charged with pressing chores and obligations elsewhere took up spades and tossed in ceremonial scoops of earth before hurrying off. Others less rushed lingered over the task of refilling the grave. Eventually, the hangers on had no more excuses to remain, and so they too returned to the day's rhythms and activities, never again to be shared by Paco. That evening Owl surprised everyone but a couple of coconspirators with a Paco Cake. He'd enlisted the aid of the senior stores manager, Gaia, and got a special dispensation of flour, nuts, dried fruit, some jealously guarded brown sugar, and some baking powder; after dinner everyone got a generous portion of Paco Cake with mint tea, thanks to Owlito.

For several days people were nervous about the source of Paco's death, especially since he hadn't done anything special or been anywhere unusual in the days leading up to his symptoms. Did that mean they were all imperiled? What unlucky sequence of factors were true for Paco, but not anyone else? (Yet?!) About all they could do was practice hygiene at higher standards than they were used to or really comfortable with. And, some would say, cultivate humility in the recognition of life's fragility.

* * * * *

Hey now, where was I?
Pages of the book on fire
Read the writing on the wall
Slowdown, it's a showdown
Everywhere you look they're fighting
Hear the call...
Well there's a change in the wind
You know the signs don't lie
Such a strange feeling
and I don't know why
It keeps taking such a long time
And you know it's getting stronger
Can't make a man much longer
Turn to stone

Turn to Stone,
Joe Walsh

They'd had an unusually warm and dry spring, which didn't bode well for their water supply later in the summer. This might not be related to the greenhouse gases we humans have been pumping into the atmosphere over the last century and a half with accelerating fossil-fuel usage, but the evidence, thanks to Al Gore and others, was very persuasive. The irony was that since the Crash, use of polluting petroleum products dropped way off. The dilemma was that even with zero use, it could take our planet up to a century to begin to return to previously experienced norms of climate cycles, say, 30 years ago.

From such a perspective, perhaps humans had for too long exceeded their carrying capacity and were about to be shed from the surviving biosphere like a snake, growing larger, splits out of and abandons its old skin. Still, with extinction as a possibility, communities of humans would try very hard to practice cooperative social techniques and simple technologies in order to extend human existence.

Regardless the cause or causes, it was hot. For now, just past the solstice, it was time to make hay, literally and figuratively. Prime growing season: If you couldn't coax something green out of the ground this time of the year, in these environs, it was time to come up with another trade, and fast. In practice, one provided sufficient water and nutrient, in a location with maximum sunlight, and the naturally occurring rhythms pretty much did the rest: light photosynthesizing into plant growth. To be sure, for optimal growth, serious soil dressing was a good idea. Whatever it is that we consume, be it leaves, flowers, seeds, the flesh around the seeds, roots or stems—or the meat raised on plants; even hypothetically, the meat raised on the meat raised on plants (carnivores)—all of it is the result of the magic of sunlight and moisture, and growth medium.

Photosynthesis converts CO_2 and H_2O into carbohydrates—starches and sugars—directly or indirectly the basic food for most of Earth's biota, and O_2, the critical molecule in the air we breathe. Furthermore, many plants draw nitrogen, an essential fertilizer, from the atmosphere and sequester it in the soil, making it available for other biota. Truly, *our friend, the plant* serves humanity in many ways.

Crow thought this over for a while in a manner that was, for him, downright reverential. And then the sensation passed and he thought about his appointment with Deke and the Stones tribe as the date approached—*I wonder if they call each other Brian, Charlie, Bill, Ron, Keith and Mick,* he idled. It was time to remind the council of this potential meeting. If the tribe could free him and a couple others from their scheduled tasks, they might make the excursion pay dividends beyond the Shovel Powwow, assuming that were really to occur. In his case, while he was in general rotation for several tasks, there were no specific, limited event he was currently signed up for; his absence for a few days would not seriously impact ongoing projects. Or so ran his thoughts in preparation for a pitch to the council.

That evening as dinner faded, the transition to council meeting was nearly seamless. With nothing significant on the agenda, Crow had the floor, *I propose that the council authorize me and a couple others to keep the rendezvous with members of the Rolling Stones...*

It's a lengthy trip when we've not had any contact with them and there's no assurance they'll even show, just to raise the obvious, Waymer said.

Quite true, Crow responded. *However, it's possible to justify this trip strictly in terms of continued foraging, and the friendly contact with this other tribe would be a bonus, should it come off. And even if there were no other contacts made, we'd still stop off at Switzerland, check in with Juan 'n' Alyshka, see what's new in our neck of the woods.*

Who were you thinking to lure away? asked Gaia.

I was hoping for a senior member; why don't you come? Crow asked Gaia, knowing she was likely too busy to leave for two nights.

No can do, buried in food preservation. You might check with Blue, though. He's pretty much unoccupied these days, she responded, with thinly disguised disapproval. Almost as an afterthought, *You* are *going to act on behalf of the Pagans, right? This isn't just a vacation toot?*

Absolutely not, he said, feigning wounded feelings. *I fully expect this trip to be proven worthwhile in terms of networking and booty. That's my aim, anyway.*

Ok, I guess you sold me. I withdraw my opposition, Waymer said.

I should point out that this trip is a kind of investment. We would need to bring some food—something beyond zucchini—to Switzerland. And we should bring some wampum, some peace offering to exchange with the Stones; I don't know what that might be, as yet, Crow slipped in.

That was very impressive, Mista Crow, exclaimed Chance, who'd intentionally sat out the earlier part of the discussion. *You managed to negotiate our approval of the bare- bones trip, then you introduced the cost, cleverly concealed in terms of "investment." Even though we didn't initially approve these add-on costs, we'd feel awkward and look pretty silly withholding support now. Especially*

154

since—I hate to say it!—these additions make perfect sense.

Despite, or perhaps because of, Crow's vigorous denials of conscious manipulation of the process, his pitch was finally approved.

Blue was indeed freer from projects needing their personal presence than nearly anyone else. He was essentially a floater: admirably participating in his duties through all his work cycles, yet not gravitating towards a niche of expertise, something other people within a decade on either side of his age tended to do. Take Gaia, for example.

Gaia, thanks to her years of health care training, was in charge of all things health related, and no one would think to challenge her expertise. Owl was another specialist: Being essentially house bound with his compromised sight, he was the house Maitre d' and peripheral cook of legendary imagination and daring. Other examples of the tendency to specialize would include Vic. While he was alive, Vic was a wizard at all things electronic. The man made them all victorious in hooking up their two solar cell panels to 12 volt DC power. Coho was the master of livestock management in life and death, which is to say, slaughtering and butchering. Chance, in his own way, orchestrated and conducted the *Dance* that was life at the

Haven. The triumvirate of Gaia, Amanita and Sparrow managed the kitchen and all things food related. All these specialties were in addition to the normal routines they were expected to share in. Chance took his turn milking, no less than Yumi, and it was a good thing Jezebel was a forgiving matron. People were encouraged to develop expertise in one or more fields, but were not thereby held exempt of everyday tasks, as a rule. Waymer made bread, as did Meadow; very similarly, in fact, the product being edible with sufficient hunger, but not particularly inspired.

Anyone could become a specialist, as a matter of choice, but no one could escape being generalist in essentially every task. In Blue's case, his "expertise" was in giving his considerable all to making up whatever deficit he encountered; his gift was being a superb generalist. He might not be the quickest, strongest, most adept at any particular skill, but very few "experts" would fail to choose Blue as their fallback person.

Yumi and Martel, having no particular skills either general or specific, were as equally uncommitted to projects as Flora at the outset. In the initial selection process for the trip, none of the three was preferable to anyone else. Until Flora made her case. She was so much more forceful in expressing her curiosity of the outside world, and so eager to experience it—while the other two were less than

convincing in communicating a desire to go al
Blue and Crow had no trouble choosing Flora.

It was a good thing they had almost a
prepare; they needed the first couple of days to come up
with the trade goods. In the end, if fresh zucchini wouldn't
do, then zucchini pancakes would have to. With four garden
mounds of several vines each, they were awash in zucchini
and summer squash; in some form or another, it would
have to be the food taken to Switzerland and packed to eat
in route. Hell, it might as well be the trading stock for the
powwow.

Owl had experimented with various ways to preserve
and prepare the currently abundant zucchini and crookneck
squash. Think Paul Simon: *Fifty ways to eat zucchini*. One
promising method was to grate, then press it, the juice
saved for soup stock or drunk with other additions, gag!
The pulp was pressed into flat discs to a thickness of about
an inch, herbed, spiced, salted, and battered before frying
in a lightly oiled skillet or toasted on a fine-mesh grill. The
range of possible spice variations made this an enduring
and endurable mid to late-summer staple. Allowed to cool
and packed carefully, zucchini pancakes could be road food
for days. Whoopee!

* * * * *

Finally, they were ready. Coyote, the nearest thing they had to being a natural mechanic, had cobbled together three mechanically-sound mountain bikes from a stock of five semi-usable ones, and parts from several others. Each bike had a basket to take some of the weight from the backpacks they'd be shouldering. These were predictably warm days but they'd need long-sleeved shirts for the cool nights. Each one brought a plastic sheet to roll up in, a small water bottle, minimal toiletries, and 5 to 6 pounds of carefully packaged, differently spiced zukecakes. Blue's were laced with dill and garlic. Flora's got taken up a notch with dried Thai chilies, and Crow's were comparatively tame with rosemary and sage. Additionally, Crow had the Glock, loaded, and an extra clip; Blue was packing a 38 revolver. They got away early afternoon after dawdling away the morning, in no particular hurry. Their plan was to stay overnight at Switzerland, and catch up on area news.

Most of the way, at least as far as Switzerland, was familiar. It was paved road except for the detours: a couple of washouts and a mud/rock/tree slide over the road. The detours could get tricky, say, at night during and after a hard rain with the creek running high. But there hadn't been any significant rain in almost a month and they expected to ford the obstacles in daylight. They started out bunched together and talking, though they gradually settled into single-file silence, Blue in the lead, maintaining a comfortable pace, on the lookout for anything suspicious ahead.

Along the way they surprised a doe and her twin 4 or 5-month olds; the three of them bounded out of sight in seconds. Further on, a tawny lynx gave their approach a baleful glare before making an unhurried retreat from the openness of the roadbed, seemingly put out by their encroachment.

They dropped down to ford the second of the washout creeks. Blue crossed dismounted with his pack and bike, leaving them on the opposite bank before returning mid-way to take Flora's pack and provide a steady hand for her traverse, Crow bringing up the rear, stepping on rocks where possible, wading in the frigid water where no stone islands appeared. Despite Blue's support, Flora slipped off a rock plunging an off-balance foot deep into the torrent, twisting an ankle in the process. Time to take a break.

They found a sunny spot along the creek side and took off their soggy shoes and socks, wringing out the socks and hanging them in the bushes. Fortunately, Flora's sprain didn't seem to be that severe, but to minimize swelling, she soaked it in the cold rushing stream, working the foot gently in and out until the foot was completely numb.

How far do you s'pose we've come? Crow asked of no one in particular.

I'd guess maybe two-thirds of the way. More than half way, for sure, ventured Blue.

With a shrug, Flora said, *No clue. Since coming to the Haven, I've only been through Switzerland once before. I sure don't remember this washout.*

Well, more important than distances to anywhere, how's that ankle feeling? Crow asked.

It's a little sore, but I think I'll be all right if I take it kinda slow.

They'd snacked on dried apple and pear slices, wiling away a half hour, Blue teasing "sure-footed Flora," while their footgear got a start at drying out. Before long, though, it was time to hit the road; it would not be a good idea to stretch out this phase of the journey, assuming Flora could continue.

Their progress thenceforward was uneventful. As they approached the opening around the Switzerland house, Crow whistled loudly; it would be rude to appear suddenly, startling Juan or Alyshka. Sure enough, Juan raised up from somesort of close gardening scrutiny, and hailed their arrival. They were doing well. By word of mouth, they'd been accepted as a sort of hub for the general area; they had become the de facto information/trading center, in addition to the bed-and-board inn they'd started with. Increased activity meant increased income in one form or another. They often had overnight guests anymore; in fact, according to Juan, a couple of "interesting" characters were also staying the night. The trio provided Alyshka with generous portions of their variously spiced zukecakes, and she was eager to learn Owl's basic recipe.

Over Alyshka's new potatoes, still-warm bread, five or six ingredients from the garden in a fresh salad, and a vegetable soup with a hint of sausage, the Pagans talked of recent events with Juan and Alyshka, and gradually got to know Rocco and Toad, two guys passing through the area looking for a place to take them in. Flora understood it was not her role to initiate discussion, and both Crow and Blue opted not to volunteer that the Pagans were basically closed to male newcomers.

After a while, growing tired of skirting the issue, Toad forced an explicit response with *How would it be for us to settle into your outfit?*

Well, it's not for us to say, offered Crow. *But the current policy, authorized by our council, states we are not taking in new residents these days.*

That sound fair to you? Toad hissed at Rocco. *They haven't even heard our long list of sterling talents,* fingering his crotch with his right hand, looking off vacantly.

Sounds like we're being shut out, is what it sounds like, Rocco growled.

You could petition the tribal council, suggested Blue. *Perhaps, if you were more specific as to the special talents?* his question dangling.

Ignoring Blue's input, *C'mon, what would it take to get us in your place?* Toad asked.

Crow tried again, a hint of exasperation in his voice, *We don't have the facilities. We can't grow enough food to support anyone else. We can't help ourselves and help you too.*

Blue tossed out without thinking, *Now, if you could grow vaginas...* and regretted it instantly .

A loud *Whoop!* from Flora, followed by unsuccessfully stifled giggles.

Hackles raised, *I ought to bust your head for that,* Rocco uttered, glowering at Blue.

As you folks know, we run a non-belligerent, strictly neutral place. There'll be no head busting here, Juan interjected, emphatically.

Backpedaling, trying to defuse the tension, Blue said, *I didn't mean anything personal; it's just that we are already loaded up with men, compared with the ladies.*

Outwardly mollified, the two sat in sullen quiet

punctuated by occasional muttering. The others talked of area events, of which, there was not much to report; apparently, no news was good news. Soon it was time for bed, and the three Pagans made their way to a vacant room upstairs. On the road like this, the sexual rotation was put on hold; everybody slept in separate beds.

The morning brought them downstairs refreshed and ready for the next stage of their journey. Though sore, Flora's ankle was not going to prevent her from continuing the adventure. Rocco and Toad had left before anyone was up, without so much as a note of appreciation. Over black tea and biscuits with honey—an incredible luxury traded by a budding beekeeper up country—they compared impressions of the evening's two other guests.

To Juan and Alyshka, *Did you ever see them before?* Blue asked.

Alyshka shaking her head as Juan answered, *Nope. No idea where they are from or where they're headed.*

They seemed fairly put out with their lot, Crow added, to heads nodding in assent. *Sorry to be the agent of disappointment to 'em.*

Not much you coulda done about it, offered Alyshka, *though I gotta say, I thought I was gonna come unglued at Blue's suggestion they grow vaginas,* initiating a new round of eye-watering peels of laughter.

Loose ends secured, the morning giving every indication that it would yield a hot day, Crow roused Blue and Flora, who were ready to go, anyway: *Let's get this row on the shoad!* They decided to bike as much of the rest of the way into the city as possible both to minimize putting weight on Flora's ankle and to permit them to cover the distance more quickly, though at heightened risk. They were hopeful they would get in more foraging around the meet up with the Stones.

They encountered a tree blown down over the road, and a couple of patches of rocks having rolled down steep embankments onto the flat surface. And some seven or eight miles out of the ghost city, they came to a massive earth-and-tree slide down a steep embankment and across the road. Since its occurrence, other travelers had need of crossing this impediment, so they simply walked their bikes over the slide on the makings of a trail established by previous travelers. By late morning, despite these obstacles, they were within the neighborhood of the powwow site, except for the season, looking very much like it had three months prior.

When they arrived at the parking lot of the TruValue Hardware store, they were greeted by still silence. They stashed the bikes deep inside the alcove of the covered loading dock and found some shade in which to cool down and consider their options. After a snack of zukecakes and no sign of their powwow co-participants, Crow asserted, *Well, this is the right day and time, and this sure is the right location...*

Maybe they got delayed and we'll be seeing them any minute, offered Flora.

And there are any number of variables that could've interfered with their coming at all, Blue added, trying to restore balance to Flora's optimism.

What do you guys think of this: Blue, you and I alternate with Flo, here, checking out the nearby shops and houses while we're waiting? asked Crow. Unstated was the understanding that Flora should not be far from one or the other of her male companions. They were packing pistols, she was not. But even if she had a weapon, alone, she would be more vulnerable than either of the men independently. Not waiting for an answer, *Does that work for you, Florita?*

Yeah, sure, no problem, she responded.

OK. It makes sense. Who goes first, asked Blue?

You choose, since it was my suggestion, said Crow.

Done! Where shall we head for first, Blossom? Blue asked.

Crow pointed out where he'd been and recommended they search the next block over, and got them to agree to check back in an hour, plus or minus. Blue and Crow each had police whistles; one blast meant to come to the source, carefully.

With his cohorts out of sight and sound, Crow sat pensively for a moment, collecting his thoughts about Deke and the Stones, beginning to doubt they would show. It was too early to say, but he supposed that something had come up. He had just about resigned himself to start systematically going through the next series of residences and street-front businesses, when he thought to check on the bicycle tires he left in the hardware stock room three months ago. Giving the building a second going over probably wasn't such a bad idea, either. His nearest access was the front of the building, the customers' entrance and exit.

If anyone had gone through the store since he'd been there, it wasn't apparent to Crow. He went over to the tipped-over wire display for seeds in hopes of finding something he might have missed before. There were, indeed, a few seed packets, mostly ornamental flowers, scattered about, all of them baring chewed holes where rodents had eaten or packed away their contents. The pint/quart/gallon paint section was intact, and he didn't have any better a reason to pack something back this time than before. On the other hand, bicycle tires had more obvious utility and would not be so much dead weight.

He walked into the occluded stock room and after a minute while his eyes adjusted to the gloom, he noted the tread of a bike tire near the edge of the top shelf. They were still here! Reflexively, he reached up and grabbed the twine loop he'd wrapped the four tires together with, three months ago. In one continuous motion, he yanked the stack of four tires—and the nest of rats, well protected inside the stack—onto himself and the floor in front of him. Momma and Poppa rat were thoroughly indignant but wasted no time retreating to a fallback sanctuary. In and amongst perhaps two cubic feet of cloth remnants, leaves and sticks, and fiberglass insulation were seven pink, squirmy thumbs, hairless, heads like little pigs, eyes not yet open.

He shook the rat turds out of his hair and brushed off his clothing while considering what to do with these protein nuggets. If they were camping, there'd be no question. *These guys would get fried, or added to the stew pot*, Crow mumbled. But they weren't staying, or building a fire. They didn't even have Jack with them; *he'd inhale them, if given the opportunity.*

He nudged a toe through the nest material to make sure there were no fugitives in hiding, then rolled the seven thumbs loosely into his bandana and put them in an outside pocket of his pack. He bounced the tires on the floor several times to free them from rodent excrement and started for the rear door.

Throwing open the door provided a flood of natural lighting, and the interior was exposed to far more visual detail; glancing around a final time, Crow now could see what looked like an old jacket hanging on a pole of somesort, propped against the back corner. On closer inspection, he could see it was the shovel with a paper wrapped around the handle, tied in place with a shoelace. He could've packed outside what was convenient and come back for the rest of his goods, but he opted to struggle out of the building bearing all his acquisitions at once, squinting at the glare and gulping the warmed air as if he'd been deprived in the darkened stock room. He found a shady spot where he could hunker down, watch the TruValue grounds, and have a swig of water. After attending to these conditions, he turned his attention to the letter attached to the shovel. It read:

> *"I see a red door and I want to paint it black*
> *no colors anymore, I want them to turn black..."*
> *Crow and fellow River Rats,* (clearly he hadn't heard of their name change)
> *Sorry to miss our powwow, but an emergency came up. By chance, a couple of our*

people were going to skirt this neighborhood the day before our meeting date (yesterday to you, if you're reading this), so I asked them to place our joint-ownership spade in a location where you could find it. A deal is a deal. I can't talk much about our emergency, inasmuch as you're not Stones members—and this could get intercepted by others. It's a security issue. We are currently evaluating the risk and developing strategies to protect ourselves from it. Is that vague enough for you?

The reason I'm telling you even this much is because, in our only conversation of perhaps five minutes, I felt a connection that I thought I could trust. I thought I was more likely to discover an ally than an adversary in getting to know you. And I hoped, while generalizing, that in your clear, fair, practical approach to the circumstances at hand, you reflected in some way the mental strength of your tribe. I hope this latter is the case, because you are apt to need all the strength and cohesion you can muster, if what we are hearing has any substance to it.

So, watch your asses and let's try this again in three months—what's that, October 15th? Hope to see you then.

Regards,

Deacon,

The Rolling Stones

July 13

If that don't goddamn beat all, Crow muttered. *He likes us all to hell, and he wants us to be on guard... against <u>what</u>? It's outrageous for him to sound an alarm and not spell out the nature of the threat, for shitsake!*

* * * * *

It was in such a state that Blue and Flora found him, lost in ruminations of illusory friendship with comrades from a different tribe. What threat or threats was Deke alluding to? Blue read the letter out loud while Flora read over his shoulder.

Well, it's clear you made a positive impression on him, Flora offered.

But what are we supposed to make of these ambiguous threats ? Blue asked.

Very perplexing, indeed, affirmed Crow. *Realistically, it's gotta be other people, doncha think?*

That sounds right; anything natural in origin—

storm damage, tree blow down, bears or cougars, forest fire, earthquakes, a sinister disease, what else could there be?—he'd be able to talk about, it seems to me, Blue said. *No hint of the supernatural, right?* a thin, satiric net cast to his meager audience.

So why can't he talk about it to us, if other people are the problem, asked Flora.

Who knows? That's the dilemma. Maybe they just don't know who poses the danger, or how extensive it is— or if there really is a danger, Crow said, shrugging. *So, what did you guys find?*

Nothing too exotic. Some shoes, socks, other clothing from a couple of houses on the next block, Blue reported. *A few rolls of TP, shampoo, bar soap; you know, the usual.*

Towels, sheets. Mostly utility stuff, Flora added. *Oh, and one little surprise that makes this trip for me. We were going to spring it on you the same time we showed it to the others.* As she spoke, Blue carefully unrolled three canning jars, pint sized, filled with gray lumps in oil. One of the lids confirmed the suspicion; the contents were tuna from summer '08.

Crow's mouth dropped, salivary glands suddenly aroused and pumping; he had to fight back the urge to devour the works, a pint for each. He was able to rein in this metabolic reaction as soon as he recognized it as an urge for selfish indulgence. Crow prided himself on his recently discovered discipline and self-denial. *Where'd you find these puppies,* he asked?

You know, they were in a cardboard box among some empty pint jars in the back of a closet of beat-up raingear, Flora said.

The benefits of looking carefully; well, good on yuz. But now, help me plan the rest of our day. It's about 3 o'clock, and won't start getting dark until 9. Do we want to stay around here overnight, or beat it back to Switzerland?

I vote to head back to Switz by this evening. The accommodations are comfortable and safe, both significant advantages over what we're likely to encounter out here, Blue reasoned.

Me too, Flora said. *Especially since our inter-tribal get together isn't happening, and we're not on a mission to find anything specific.*

That sounds good to me. But what say to another hour or so of foraging? Crow asked. *I got an empty satchel and I haven't had a crack at the treasure hunt this time.*

Sure. Let's go back to where we left off, Blue suggested, Flora nodding beside him.

For the next hour and a half, the trio searched six

houses. They found more shoes, too many to bring back, allowing them to be far more selective in size and type of shoes to be packed home. They found a vast array of kitchen and dining accoutrements, again requiring them to choose carefully. Large bowls were always a premium, serving triple duty as food gathering containers, meal preparation, and meal service. Special attention had to be paid to the material of the bowl. Stainless was virtually indestructible, but had zero warmth or class. On the other hand, on more than one occasion a ceramic bowl of some distinction had failed to survive the journey home, or had had a brief career, once arrived.

Blue located a large hand-thrown stoneware bowl and was hunting for towels and other clothing as packing for another attempt at bringing back an attractive as well as utilitarian bowl. If he succeeded, he'd be lauded; if he failed, he'd be teased for being so foolish as to think he could transport such a fragile thing so crudely. Crow found a case of empty quart canning jars, which he filled, each one, with laundry detergent, screwing down the lids before returning them to the cardboard carton. It was an awkward bulk but it would fit in his backpack with sufficient clothing to cushion the edges. The trick was to not get overloaded, a phenomenon Flora had succumbed to.

The ability to recognize and pack accordingly no

more than you could comfortably carry *over distance*—as opposed to the brute strength required for only four or five minutes—came with practice, and Flora had been on a foraging excursion only once before. Either Blue or Crow could have commented on the sheer volume she planned to take back and it would've had the force of an imperative. But each came to the conclusion that it would be an interesting experience to watch Flora teach herself, learn empirically, what she could reasonably pack, on and off a bicycle, some 15 miles back to Switzerland. By the second time she signaled for a stop, Crow tried offering pragmatic encouragement, *If you don't mind, let's see what all you got there.*

Out of the top the pack came a nearly unbroken stream of clothing in and amongst several pairs of shoes, sheets, and the occasional curiosity: a softball and a couple of frizbees. Three trashy romance novels. A small makeup kit. *Hello! What's up with that?* Crow asked.

I don't know, just something to play with, I guess. I used to like to get myself all done up, Flora said.

Do <u>me</u> a favor and toss the makeup kit. And we'll talk about whether it was the right decision—revisit the lure of former decadence—at a council when we get back. Do <u>yourself</u> a favor and dump even more—at least one of those books, and a couple pairs of shoes. And cull 10 to

20% of the rest.

Flora sulked for a while, glancing at Blue, hoping for sympathy. His response was to give a half shake of the head, as if to say, *He's right; you got way too much stuff there.*

Crow understood, in this instance, that he had set himself up as the heavy, so he told them he was going on ahead slowly; they were to catch up. Blue had no more sympathy for Flora's plight than Crow but he was obliged to bring up the rear. He offered to carry one small item that she would otherwise have to pitch, if it would soften the blow. And promote moving along.

She practically beamed until Blue said, *But not the makeup kit*...When she'd recovered her composure, contrite, she settled on one of the abandoned pairs of shoes.

Our Little Flower still has a taste for that Big City opulence, he mused, stuffing the gaudy platform shoes into his pack.

* * * * *

As known quantities, the natural obstacles seemed less daunting on the way back. It was around sunset, maybe eight o'clock, when they arrived at Switzerland to encounter a distraught Alyshka. It had been a normal day, normal routine through midday when Juan told her he was going to take the barrow and bring back a load of firewood from the woodlot he was taking from out east of there. She continued working the garden—a real handful these long, hot days, what with watering, bringing in the harvest, and staying on top of the preservation process. It wasn't unusual for Juan to be gone for two hours or more, and she had more than enough to occupy her attention. But as the afternoon wore on, she had started to wonder. By mealtime, she was sure something was amiss. Unless he told her explicitly, he was always back by evening mealtime, usually before, to give her a hand. Juan was not shy around the kitchen and was a serviceable cook, himself, within a finite range of recipes.

There were no other Switzerland guests that night. With at least an hour's daylight left, Crow and Blue set off in the direction of the woodlot while Flora stayed with Alyshka. Before leaving, in a brief aside out of Alyshka's hearing, Crow asked Flora to see if Alyshka would talk about her relationship with Juan: How were they getting along; anything unusual going on recently, that sort of thing.

Several hundred yards east of the house, they were in younger second growth that showed signs of having been thinned. The deeper into that copse they ventured, the less thinned the forest appeared. They had separated 20-or-so feet on either side of the main trail and were taking it rather slowly so as to not miss anything—evidence that Juan, or anyone else, had been there, signs of a fight, anything. They withheld calling out to Juan, thinking he might have been waylaid and his captors were waiting for their appearance; both men thought there was a possible connection to Rocco and Toad's acrimonious stay the previous night.

A little farther along on Blue's side of the trail, they discovered the wheelbarrow turned on its side but otherwise, nothing. So he'd come that far. But no Juan. No tools, no wood, nothing else there; what the hell was going on? They could walk out on the trail in near-total darkness, so they decided to press on a while longer. A half hour later, light fading, they gave up for the night, leaving the barrow where they'd found it. They'd resume the next day where they left off the search; it would all look different in the morning light.

They returned to the women preparing dinner—ubiquitous and seemingly eternal zucchini cakes and a big salad straight out of the garden. Keeping busy in the kitchen appeared to keep Alyshka distracted, though she was conspicuously harried and manic about it. Flora was helping out with cleanup when Crow and Blue walked in. They explained that they'd found the wheelbarrow but nothing else. They'd scouted the area but had to give up because of impending darkness.

Nothing else? Alyshka echoed.

We'll be able to look more thoroughly in the morning, but we didn't find anything unusual. And we scoured the vicinity of the wheelbarrow real good, Blue offered apologetically, Crow nodding agreement. It was a tricky situation, one in which they were sorry they didn't find Juan, say, moderately injured or incapacitated, to account for his absence, but secretly glad not to have found him dead, he thought.

Alyshka nodded stoically and daubed her eyes. *Well, something's happened to 'im; he had no cause to just run away,* she trailed off.

The atmosphere over dinner was morose, with feeble attempts at constructing positive morning outcomes on the part of the Pagans, and scant participation by Alyshka. They carried on through hot teas and meal clean up, but soon it became clear there was no reason to stay up any longer. They were all wrung out; the Pagans, at least, would go to sleep quickly this night. After confirming there was nothing else they might do for Alyshka, they said their goodnights.

In the privacy of their upstairs room, the two men quizzed Flora as to how Alyshka seemed; what was her overall mood? Anything unusual? Flora hadn't noticed a thing out of the ordinary, based on putting herself in Alyshka's shoes and accounting for the different life-experiences, personalities, etc. Flora had met Juan and Alyshka passing through on her first scavenging trip, but based on these few hours together with her in obvious stress—well, she quickly felt a great deal more sympathy and respect for Alyshka.

That's pretty much how I felt about them both, Crow said. *I haven't seen anything yet to make me doubt my feeling.*

No arguments out of me on these folks, concurred Blue. *Tomorrow, we'll continue the search. We'll find him if he's out there.*

And I don't see any reason why we all shouldn't go, Crow added. *But here's the thing: I want her coming with us to be her decision. I expect she'll want to come, but if she wants to stay, do you mind staying with her again?* looking at Flora.

Well, I was hoping to be part of the search... But I'm the logical one to stay with her. And I'm glad for the chance to build the connection, Flora said, putting a positive spin on that contingency.

Morning came all too soon. Blue was up at dawn to get a fire going and get some water heating. However, Alyshka was up earlier, or still up, looking even more gaunt and haggard than the night before, though she was more communicative and outwardly appreciative of their presence.

I can't thank you guys enough for being here, she said.

Say no more about it, Crow said. *We're glad to be able to help. What are your thoughts on this morning's search?*

Oh, I want to go too. It's ok that I come along, isn't it?

Sure, we'll all go, Crow said. *What do you need to do before we head out?*

Not much. Hang the "Come in and make yourself at home, we'll be back soon" *sign on the front door and put my boots on...*Around breakfast, they'd re-cooked most of the zukecakes to extend their nutritive function, and they would pack at least a pound each for adequate if boring sustenance.

Five minutes out, they spread out 15 feet apart or so, men on the outside to help set the pace, which was slow. Blue and Crow, by example, discouraged talking on the theory that it distracted your attention; Flora and Alyshka, however, but mostly Flora, did not hesitate to demonstrate they were capable of both activities simultaneously. When they got to the wheelbarrow, they spent some time fanned out in all directions looking for any evidence of human presence. After a while, all returned to the barrow from their fruitless search, Alyshka being the last. Nobody had found anything remotely suspicious or out of the ordinary.

I can't do this, Alyshka said in a choked voice. *I thought I could, but this is too hard.*

Don't worry about it, Flora said. *This isn't as much fun as I thought, either,* the malaprop irony allowed to fade unchallenged. Then, offered more modestly, *I'll walk back with you.*

Before they left, Crow gave Flora his 9mm semi-automatic. She had practiced and could hit a human target at close range, if need be. He'd rely on Blue's weapon for the rest of their search. *Expect us by late afternoon,* Crow said to the departing women.

As the women walked out of sight, Crow and Blue extended their break. Blue was first to speak, *Something's funny about this, doncha think?*

I don't follow; something about Alyshka?

No, not her at all. It's this place. If this is where he was headed with the barrow, and he got hijacked or something, I think we'd see the results of a struggle.

Yeah, you're right, Crow agreed. *Either he left willingly, or the struggle took place somewhere else.*

...And in both cases, the placement of the barrow is

a red herring! Blue added. *We've devoted far too much attention to this place; we should move along.*

Resuming the pattern they'd established the night before, Crow said, *You realize, if Juanito left of his own accord, we'll likely never find any sign of where he went.*

Yeah, I thought of that. In the meantime, let's look for something that tells us there was a fight.

Within a couple hundred yards beyond the barrow, what had been a fairly uniform trunk of the trail, in the pattern of game trails, began to drift and wander and separate as the valley flattened out, still mostly conifer, some deciduous. Another fifty yards and it was impossible to tell which tributary represented the main trail—the elk freeway. They continued on what they thought was the general direction of the interlaced trails, looking from side to side for anything out of the ordinary. This network of trails was clearly common access to/from other places, based on the amount of deer, but mostly elk, droppings and their hoof prints. Conspicuously, there was *no* sign of foot or boot prints, no horses.

Not a goddamn thing tells us a human's been through here, Blue mused. *Or to invert that, everything we've seen tells us no human came this way.* Little by little, the terrain changed from an open, spread out, basin area to a more defined trail as it followed the easiest way up some hilly country and through the saddle of the pass, on its way into the next watershed. The two men stopped at a shady spot in the saddle. Midday or a little after, it was a good place for a break and a review of their objectives.

After a few minutes for a drink of water and a snack of zukecakes spent in reflection and quietude, Blue got right to it, *Where are we going?*

And its corollary, Why did we come this far? Crow responded.

Oh, it's a pleasant enough walk, but now's not a particularly good time for it. And neither of us has seen so much as a footprint that wasn't our own. We aren't pros at tracking but we're reasonably observant, and it's hard to imagine someone could avoid leaving footprints here and there. It's safe to say no hominid has been through this area in the last few weeks.

Yeah, I hate to admit it but you're right, Crow conceded. *I kept thinking we'd come upon something just beyond that bend in the trail, just through this thicket, in the next 50 yards...*

But not forever, right? This might seem like the logical way to us, but we can't make it be the way, no matter how much we think it should be. Time to reassess. Nothing leads to nothing.

There was nothing to reassess. They'd gone beyond

normal follow-through in determining neither Juan nor anyone else had come this way recently. They would go back now, taking a slightly different, parallel set of trails, retrieving the barrow on the way. Perhaps they'd missed a stealthy cross-trail some distance before they came on the barrow; in any event, for now they had no answer to the mystery.

On the way, they talked about one of them going back to the Haven with Flora; their fellow Pagans would start to be concerned by this evening, and there was no reason for two of them to stay any longer. The remaining person, however, should stay a few more days. To be a helper, companion, and protector, if it came to that, until someone else showed up to fill in. They talked about it; neither of them felt very strongly either way about it: Who would stay with Alyshka, and who would return with Flora?

Finally, though neither could say what the decision turned on, it was agreed that Blue would stay; a Pagan would come to replace him by the third day midday, unless he appeared by the second evening, meaning Juan had miraculously returned, or someone from a different community had come to help out.

It was, indeed, mid-afternoon by the time they got back to the Switzerland homestead. Flora was reading, ensconced in a rocking chair, while Alyshka dozed on the futon sofa in the common room. Blue and Crow's arrival, though moderately quiet, unfortunately roused Alyshka from her fitful sleep.

She would've been better off continuing her sleep; there was no benefit to hearing sooner rather than later perhaps the most agonizing of news—there was simply nothing to tell.

* * * * *

PART IV

Out here in the fields
I fight for my meals
I got my back into my living

I don't need to fight
to prove I'm right
I don't need to be forgiven...

Baba O'Riley,
The Who

from Waymer's journal account:

7/04: There's a curious ambivalence about this day, the birthday of America, her self-emancipation from the yoke of England. Most of us have fond memories of hot summer picnics and fireworks and the exquisite lethargy of the season. I'm a naturalized citizen; I wasn't born here, so I became a citizen through choice and effort. Nevertheless, I don't think a single one of us Pagans is sorry to see ol' Merka dissolve, presumably, accompanied by most other nation-state entities. Implode from their own greed-driven excesses. In fact, one could posit human/biosphere suffering might have been lessened, had the implosion happened sooner.

Still, none of that prevents me from thinking of the Fourth of July a little wistfully. It was a landmark in the national landscape, a canon of cannons, noise and skyrockets, a part of my acquired-culture identity. I didn't have to like what it had come to represent in order to have a good time on a holiday with my buds. Hot, languid days tempered with cold beer, reefer, and the local blues festival. Invariably, nightfall brought a three-quarter hour display of staccato, colorful, noisy, air-polluting Chinese rocket explosives.

Was there ever such a society whose citizens liked to crash things, or blow them up, as much as Merkans did? Feature limitless vehicular destruction in Hollywood's *action cinema*? Exult in the bloodletting of extreme sports? Promote contests in which people compete to see how many hot dogs, hard-boiled eggs, raw oysters—pick your poison—you can eat within a time frame. What a country!

7/09: Before there was money as an exchange of commonly accepted value, there was the barter system. But since nobody places any value on US legal tender anymore, we have returned to a very subjective weighing of the relative need vs. means of payment of any good or service—the essence of barter. It's very personal, intense transacting. Some have taken hours before they were consummated. Recently, via the Switzerland message board, our intrepid negotiators were able to trade some tool duplicates and two gallons of kerosene for a handful of chickens, and a nanny goat and her two month-old kids; we've catapulted into animal husbandry! Coho is our point person on caring for/ managing livestock, but despite his best efforts, this may have been too big an undertaking all at once.

Needless to say, Jack, our protective mutt, is truly perplexed. He takes his job seriously and believes himself to be a vigilant guard against potential interlopers of various species. One imagines him thinking, *It looks like I'm being asked to accept these inferior, prey animals into the family. On top of the sufferance of the lay-about cat, this is a canine indignity of the greatest magnitude!* Now he walks around sniffing them trying to discern what makes them worthy. The chickens have figured out he's been domesticated and pretty much ignore him. But Jezebel, our newly-christened nanny goat, takes a horned swing at him whenever she gets the chance.

7/10: The chicken coop and enclosure took some fidgeting to get in order, which we finally managed; the only way to insure chickens' survival is to keep them completely enclosed at night, since nocturnal denizens the likes of raccoons and skunks would make short work of them, otherwise. But the goddamn goats are gonna ruin us! We confine them at night too, of course, the kids in one enclosure, Jezebel in the other. We milk her first thing in the morning, and the kids can suckle all day long. During the day, if they are not confined or trussed very securely, and sometimes even if they are, they require monitoring every waking moment. They can and will get into more places, eat more plants in a shorter time frame than you would have imagined possible. They stripped the leaves off of two fairly big rose bushes in about three minutes, from a starting point of maybe a 100 yards away, them circuitously munching the whole devious approach. They've set back the raspberries, young fruit trees...Meanwhile, these goats have managed to charm most of us with their curious, playful antics, especially the kids. Personally, I think it's a ruse to hide their inherent deviousness—with a highly developed sense of smell. In a fugitive moment, Jezebel and her kids were homing in on some exotic leafy-green, about to tuck into our patch of cannabis, when fortunately they were caught at the last moment. Or there would have been wholesale capricide, no mistake. It's enough to give thoughts of a consolation celebration of our failed experiment of goat herding with—you guessed it— barbecued goat!

<u>7/17</u>: Two of our intrepid intertribal trade trio returned last night (Crow and Flora, with Blue staying behind) reporting the disappearance of Switzerland's host, Juan, made the more troubling in that no one could come up with a reasonable explanation for it. The intended goal of our team was to powwow in the city with the Rolling Stones, another tribe. Via a chance encounter with some of their members three months ago, Crow established a connection and an agreement to a follow-up meeting, on the pretext of retrieving a shovel both parties claimed, but agreed to

alternating possession. Unfortunately, the *Dirty Beatles* were unable to attend, owing to their own unspecified complications, although they made good on their agreement, leaving the Spade of Contention, along with a note.

But our primary concern, of course, falls to Alyshka and the situation at Switzerland. Aside from being a thoroughly likeable couple, Juan and Alyshka's courage in establishing a safe house/way station has won them admiration far and wide. Their facility has burgeoned into an information-and-trading hub, so popular have they become these few short months. Their loss would be a terrible setback to the region.

As an aside, our sojourners brought back satchels of loot from their time going through derelict shops and former dwellings, underscoring that, even at this late date, foraging continues to pay dividends.

7/19: Blue came back this afternoon. By way of people passing through Switzerland, the word's spread about Juan turning up missing, and there's been a flow of support from all directions. Blue stayed an extra night meeting folks who came to stay a few days, having brought fresh garden edibles and already-prepared goods as well. Alyshka reports that the ongoing pain she feels of not knowing what happened to her Juanito is like an open wound. Still, she is holding up, thanks to all the people who showed up to lend a hand. As yet, she claims she has no desire to move.

From Blue's estimation, there must be a lot more of these subsistence-farm experiments than the half dozen we'd imagined, based on the outpouring of area support. A postscript to Blue's accomplishments: he was able to make it all the way back without breaking a substantial trophy, a large, handsomely glazed ceramic bowl. He's apt to get a fat head from all the kudos heaped upon him.

7/23: Our garden flourishes, despite the occasional capricious depredations. Our attempt at carbohydrate cultivation—a big area in potatoes, bigger in soybeans, some experimental patches of oats, barley, wheat—comes along slowly. A small plot of peanuts in an area of full sun; I can almost taste our own homemade peanut butter! Makes you wet your pants in anticipation.

What a great pleasure it is (I never thought I'd say that!) eating straight out of the garden—or mediated only slightly via the kitchen. These days I find myself discovering, or recognizing a connection to the land, to the cycle of life, that goes beyond mere understanding; this seems to be perceived more on a subconscious than volitional level. Others are experiencing it too. One's labors yield such sustaining bounty; one sees the connection in earth-caked hands, sun-tanned arms and backs, and rediscovered muscles. The Hindus refer to it as *Prana*, I believe: the free-floating, inter-connected energy of life that you fleetingly have awareness of. It's a giddy feeling.

7/25: Increasingly, we're trying to preserve food for the off months. Thin-sliced apples and pears, as well as most of the wild berries through the summer can be dried on wire mesh. A venison ham and a couple of salmon slow smoked over alder and native cherry woodchips. Some plums dried, but, by popular acclaim, the bulk *fermented!* Gearing up for phases of canning, starting with cucumber pickles, then green beans and tomatoes, chunked or cooked down as sauce. We'll put up some *salsa picante* also. Do you realize, if we only used one canned quart jar a day (for the whole family!), that would take at least 275 canned quarts! We might have 150 or so. No matter, we Pagans will thrive!

7/26: The milking crew was finishing up coaxing a miserable pint out of Jezebel and Jack had been putting up an awful racket—*pretty persistent deer! Or four, maybe five elk*, Yumi and Coho were thinking —when a stranger appeared, out of the literal gray. They were plenty spooked until they got a good look at him. A middle-aged man, he was badly beaten up, shaking, and incoherent. A big wound skirted his left eye, very swollen and bruised, and he was cradling his likely-broken left arm. So they brought him inside, cleaned him up a bit, and got some hot tea into him. Meanwhile, Yumi made the rounds sounding the alarm. The group of people in current security rotation had to scramble to head out to points around our perimeter to check for activity. And at least a couple of elders need to interrogate the refugee. I'm off on patrol for a couple hours.

(Later) Nothing out of the ordinary on Gaia and my patrol; so far, no news is good news as to the other patrols. We've learned some things from our surprise guest, though. After an hour or so of friendly faces, warm food, and warm environment our visitor, Taybo, began to tell his story. He is from Three Farms, a small group of farms in the same neighborhood some 17, 18 miles down valley, by way of the crow. They were taken unaware by maybe 20 raiders in 4 vehicles; they just drove up and shot anyone who resisted. Their plunder was food, intoxicants, fuel, and anything that drew their attention, especially the females. Without weapons, unprepared to resist, he and ultimately the rest of the living surrendered.

Yesterday evening he was loaded in the back of a stake-sided pickup with 14 other males, no room to sit down, and driven out of their valley. Believing they were being taken away somewhere to be shot, he and two others jumped off the back of the 20-mph-pickup and rolled down an embankment. The other two got up and were trying to make it to some tree cover when they were picked off with bursts of automatic weapon fire. Though Taybo was badly hurt from the tumble, he lay very still. After a few minutes, they drove off. He walked all night over cross-country terrain with scant moon and starlight in search of shelter. And to warn us.

7/27: By Taybo's account, these raiders' m.o. is to overrun a settlement, kill off all resistance, slaughter and eat all the livestock, eat or haul off all the food on hand, and kill or take away the womenfolk. Before they leave, they torch what remains. Scorched earth.

Chance's sardonic reply on hearing these particulars, instantly the stuff of legend: *I guess that rules out negotiation!*

Time for our long-practiced self-defense strategy to kick in. Until we deem it safe, every adult is to have a firearm and ammo with him/her at all times. Nonessential tasks are curtailed and those freed up pairs/trios are to help maintain defense positions, particularly along the main road access, since that was how Three Farms got raided. At the same time, a smaller group, headed by Amanita and including the juvies, shuttles portions of food, clothing, bedding, some cooking gear, weapons, fuel, in short, everything of value, to a couple of caches well hidden in the forest as much as a half mile away from the house. Anticipating such a threat, 55-gallon steel drums had been buried in strategic locations months prior; these containers are able to house moisture-sensitive goods for just such an occasion: perishables, clothing, and weapons/ammunition could be kept safe in such a way indefinitely.

The plan is to defend the Haven, assuming we get some advance warning; try to catch them in crossfire along the entry road as they approach. Then fall back on both sides, resisting their advance to the house. But not at all costs. With nothing strategic, or even supportive, left in the house, we hope to make it more of a trap than a conquest. We want to minimize our casualties, maximize theirs, favoring skirmishes and ambushes— guerrilla tactics. Blue and Coho are practiced snipers, so they will pick 'em off till it gets dark. Then we bide our time: wait till they're all asleep, even if they've posted sentries until, say, around 3 am. At which time we sneak in very quietly and kill 'em all. Maybe dynamite a couple of their vehicles. It ain't fancy but that's the plan, according to the council mandate.

7/28: While this plan had some appeal based on its stark,

acetic simplicity, its minimalist approach, people just as readily fault it for being watery thin in specific detail. We know of two other communities more-or-less between Three Farms and us and we are quite anxious as to their fate. In any event, these marauders seem to be working in our general direction, scouring the countryside as they come.

7/31, midday: It's getting painful maintaining high alert. The tendency is to be more and more complacent as the hours and days pass by and nothing happens. This is the third day of high alert and some malcontents are beginning to call for a review of the threat level and a return to "normal" summer activities. We are losing these golden days and they won't be back, many of them, for another year.

* * * * *

Oh, a storm is threat'ning
my very life today
If I don't get some shelter
oh yeah, I'm gonna fade away
War, children,
it's just a shot away,
it's just a shot away
Rape, murder!
It's just a shot away,
shot away,
shot away...

Gimme Shelter,
The Rolling Stones

That hot, sunny, listless afternoon of Waymer's last journal entry, the raiders appeared and blew the Pagans' waiting-for-action limbo to kingdom come. These were Vikings in land ships, Mongols astride mechanical horses, thundering in their approach. The advance guard along the road heard them coming maybe two minutes before they were in view. Two long, shrill blasts on a police whistle sounded the alarm. Two minutes to get to battle stations.

As anticipated, there were four vehicles; two pickups, a van and a sedan, four to six people per rig. As anticipated, the defenders rained bullets on the cavalcade, inflicting casualties. What wasn't anticipated was how fast they would be moving, racing through the corridor, so as to minimize exposure, right up to the roadblock, preventing their advance. In the early days of the group, they realized how vulnerable they were by road. As a result, they built a formidable obstacle of large boulders and various riprap, all cabled together and located strategically where mixed forest growth gave way to the homestead clearing.

Forced to stop, these latter-day highwaymen poured out of their rigs and ran for cover, encountering Martel with the AK-47, and Sparrow and Amanita with rifles, intent on slowing their advance. He sprayed them from the time they stopped, pausing only to replace empty clips, until there were no longer any targets—at least four dead or badly wounded, and the rest well concealed.

At which point the three of them began to fall back in an orderly, protected manner. Except that briefly, Sparrow paused, semi-concealed, involved in reloading, and was fumbling it somewhat. It was a moment of vulnerability, and she practically got caught. Twenty yards away, an invader saw his chance and pounced. Approaching quickly, he was a full stride away from grabbing her when one of the snipers took out the threat with a lucky shot through the neck. Coho had been aiming for the upper torso and had shot a little high. Writhing, the man died strangling, drowning in his own blood. Sparrow made a quick wave in the direction of the rifle discharge, grabbed the fallen man's weapon, and dashed for deeper cover.

In the free-fire melee contesting the house, Tooloose was killed outright, a bullet through his head. Then Jack, their beloved companion and watchdog, had a long, heart-wrenching death. Scrambling to reach forest protection, pulling back from the vicinity of the house with the others, but not quite as quick, Chance took a shot through the lower abdomen. The impact knocked him down and caused him to struggle to breathe; concentrating his energy on the task of sitting up was all he could manage before they were on him. Rather than end his trial on the spot, two of the raiders dragged him the forty feet or so back to the house while their confederates provided supporting bursts of gunfire. He was hauled inside and propped up, leaning against a wall, grimacing in pain.

One of their lieutenants brought him a cup of water. *Where'd your friends go?* he asked.

I guess you ran 'em off, he winced, a dark stain

steadily soaking an expanding circle of shirt around the entry wound in his lower torso, that side of his pants now wet also.

I guess we did, at that, the man snickered.

You know we're gonna win. We are guardians of culture, its reinterpretation, Chance gasped. *You are parasites of culture. We help bear civilization but you are civilization's destroyer.*

Ha! You hear that, Chigger? He's a "guardian of culture!" interjected the second man with a airy guffaw. *This ol' boy's got a lip on 'im, don't he?*

You can win battles but you cannot win the war, Chance now desperately reaching to catch his breath. In a final effort, he hissed, *People need connection with each other, crave community. When culture gets trampled under, it springs back, irrepressible. A Phoenix reborn from its own...* the pain audible, gasped, *goddamn...* gurgled now, *ashes...*then, very slowly, he sagged to one side and was gone.

* * * * *

The raiders had assumed their appearance would come as a total surprise, as in previous raids, and that overpowering any resistance and subduing the rest would come at little cost. Not only had they lost something like half their contingent in gaining the house, they were now under siege. There were virtually no "spoils" to celebrate, the house being, except for furniture, essentially barren—a totally unforeseen outcome. Also unanticipated was their failure to capture at least one hostage, and that recognition was also dawning on tribal members, arrayed in concealed positions surrounding the buildings.

Jezebel and one of her daughters had been spirited away during the final withdrawal but in the haste and confusion, the other kid was left behind. In a lull of the commotion, mindless of the human drama around her, starting to miss her mother and sister, bleating, calling to them, she ventured into the open where she was promptly shot. When one of the invaders strode out to retrieve the carcass, he too was badly wounded from two directions of fire. He lay there in plain sight of the house occupants, alternately whimpering and crying out, pleading for help, and eventually cursing his comrades for abandoning him. The invaders were clearly pinned in a house with no food and no water—unseen Pagans had earlier unplugged the house water system.

With the gathering darkness, pairs and trios of Pagans made the rounds to each sentry post in the circle surrounding the buildings. They first established that their comrades were unhurt, then rallied them with some stockpiled rations, more ammunition, water, and a jacket against the advancing evening. They exchanged what information each member had, and in the case of Amanita and Yumi, relieved them of their posts.

Afterward, regrouping, the consensus was that, besides Tooloose, Chance was also probably dead, either of his initial wound or succumbing to mistreatment after being hauled inside. Otherwise, even these lowlifes would have realized by now they could use him in somesort of hostage deal. Jack, too, was dead. And Jezebel's nanny kid. Miraculously, however, their only other casualty was Flora, who'd had a bullet nick the top of her left shoulder; she was in pain, but her injury was not life threatening.

For their part, the raiders' losses were a confirmed eleven with the likelihood of at least a couple more wounded inside. In their zeal to capture the house and other buildings, the invaders had left the vehicles unguarded, some forty yards of mostly open space away. Earlier, when two of them had tried to return to the vehicles, they were cut down in withering fire. With twenty, maybe twenty-three invaders at the outset, the Pagans were feeling better about their odds.

A short debate ensued as to how to retake their home and what to do about the vehicles. Blue, quickly emerging as their best strategist, spoke: *Come nightfall, they're likely to make a run for the vehicles, doncha think?*

Yeah, that's what I'd do if I were in their shoes, said Waymer.

No matter what, we can't let them get away, chimed in Amanita.

You betcha! We don't want a single one of these shitheads to escape, only to come back for another "visit," affirmed Coho.

So, let's disable the rigs, said Blue. *Pull sparkplug wires, take the keys if they left 'em, remove a wheel; whatever it takes, they can't drive out of here.*

And shoot the dirty dogs to hell; kill 'em all, Amanita uttered with uncharacteristic ferocity.

Alright, then. Since it's unlikely they'll strike out in an unfamiliar direction, especially at night, let's pull every other sentry from the perimeter and send them to road defense and vehicle dismantling detail, said Blue, warming to his new-found role. *I'll head clockwise; Waymer or Coho, one of you head counter-clockwise, and we'll meet up on the other side of their rigs in 15, 20 minutes.*

I'm good for it, Waymer said, knowing he was more rested than Coho.

One more suggestion: Why don't a couple folks build a big bonfire off west, there, below the tree line? Within sight of the house?

What the fuck for? asked Coho.

It's just an idea, and plenty dangerous at that. It'll give these assholes something to ponder—a distraction, if you will. While we fuck with their rigs and set the trap.

Yeah, ok. I guess that makes sense. In a kind of non-sensical way, allowed Coho.

Just be goddamn careful once you light it, is all. Stay out of the light and avoid being an easy target; they may have binocs, for all we know.

A suicidal diversion, eh? Right up my alley, said Coho.

Off we go, then. Oh, and tell everybody to converge on the buildings, once you hear two long blasts of the whistle. Shoot to disable.

Twenty minutes later, six of them reassembled behind the rigs in the near darkness: Blue, Waymer, Sparrow, Crow, Martel, and Yumi. Crow and Waymer, Martel tagging along, got busy going from rig to rig. In one case, disconnecting the battery, in another two, taking the keys after locking the steering wheel. Removing sparkplug wires on the last two. Soon the vehicles were inoperable. By now it was quite dark. As prearranged, they all took positions of cover between the buildings and the vehicles and waited. And waited. Their best-case scenario, that of having all the invaders walk into the trap at once, was beginning to look like it was a non-starter.

Non-starter... *Wait a minute*, thought Blue. *If these assholes won't come on their own, maybe they need a little inducement, something to lure them.* Waymer kept the keys to these rigs, right? He walked quietly to the nearest sentry. *Martel, pass the word. Send back the vehicle keys. I'm gonna start one; see if I can't flush 'em out.*

As luck would have it, one set of keys fit the sedan, the one pointing in the general direction of the house. Sure enough, Blue no sooner started the engine of the sedan than several men came out of the house, fumbling with boots and weapons, before setting out to rescue their rig. They'd covered about half the distance, their nervous voices and the muffled engine idle the only sound, when Blue, crouching in the back seat, carefully reached around the driver's seat and flipped on the headlights.

Six invaders quickly dissolved the huddle they'd formed coming that far. Surprised, profane exclamations were uttered while shooting at the idling car, its headlights mercilessly exposing them to the hail of bullets coming from cover around them. They finally shot out the lights but by then, it didn't matter. Blue turned off the ignition and shouted, *Hold your fire. Keep your positions.* The whole battle could not have lasted a minute, probably more like forty-five seconds, the cacophony now replaced by silence.

Almost complete silence. Some low moaning and erratic scraping coming from the battleground were the only sounds.

Keeping covered as much as possible, Blue made the rounds to see how everybody was. *Unscathed.* They pulled back to a place better-protected from the house. Quieter now. Did we think they were all dead? *Not likely.* How to make sure? *Very carefully.* Crow and Martel volunteered to give their casualties a once over; a living-but-disabled invader could provide intelligence.

I'm going too, Yumi said. *Another handgun and pair of eyes might be useful.*

They took one of the two functioning flashlights, knowing that to use it in sight of the house was to invite being shot. Crow said, *As quiet as we can make this, follow my lead,* and set off approaching the battle area.

The first person they encountered was quite dead, as were the second and third, splayed in awkward poses. The fourth was barely alive, presumably from loss of blood; since he was beyond communicating, he was disarmed and "set aside," a euphemism for "allowed to bleed out." The fifth man, Caucasian, probably late 20s, was alive, though very cold to the touch, and barely responsive. Likely, in shock.

Yumi confirmed the death of number six by stepping

on an arm in the dark and tripping over the rest of him. The whole instant-fear-to-surreal-incongruity triggered at first sniggers, soon reinforced by Martel's guilty, irrepressible snort. At which time, nothing was going to hold it back; the flood gates were loosed, and they surrendered to waves of uncontrollable laughter. Crow too lapsed into hysteria; it was unjustifiable, unexplainable, and wholly out of place, but there they were rolling around giggling, chortling, guffawing, teary eyed, as if they'd all succumbed to a rousing jolt of lysergic acid diethylamide.

Crow and Martel, once they'd recovered their composure, helped their bewildered captive hobble to a safe location. He was shot through a thigh—a shattered femur but no arterial bleeding. There they helped him sit down, and gave him a blanket and some warm tea, for which he was very grateful. Then they handcuffed his hands behind his back.

What's your name, Blue asked?

The guy looked at him but didn't say anything.

You take these things in benign, incremental steps. *Look, my name is Blue. You're going to have to help us out here. Telling me your name isn't that big a deal, is it? No state secrets tied up in your name?*

Once again the guy looked at him. Then looked away before mumbling, *Robbie.*

What? I didn't catch that.

The name's Robbie, quite clearly this time.

Thank you, Robbie. It's a pleasure to make your acquaintance. I'm sure you know you've got a nasty leg wound, there. You're pretty much out of commission, as far as pillaging peaceful farms out in the countryside. But exactly how you spend the rest of your days is going to depend on how you answer the next few questions. Are you paying attention, Robbie? Here we go: How many people rode in here with you?

Long pause while the prisoner seemed to consider his fate. *This is not going well, Robbie,* nudging the toe of his shoe at the man's wound.

Involuntary gasp and shooting pain, like firecrackers, exploding in his brain. After a few seconds, Blue again made a gesture with his foot in the direction of the wound and the man cried out, a little too loud, *22! There were 22 of us.*

Very good, Robbie. See how easy this can be? Ok, how many dead or seriously wounded you got up in the house?

No hesitation now. *Four dead, counting your guy, and one shot through the lower back. Alive and very unhappy.*

Leaving, what, two more-or-less able-bodied

people?

Yeah, I think so. I don't actually know for sure.

Ok, Robbie the Robber Raider, Robbie the Rabid Rabbit, we're going to cuff you to a tree back here out of the way while we check your numbers...

Please, no! I'm hurt; I can't go anywhere...

Like I was saying, Robert, if you behave yourself and keep quiet, we'll discuss what your good behavior gets you. You do want to be part of the discussion, don't you? The discussion of your fate?

Despite his pain and acute discomfort, Robbie submitted to his only chance at survival; he was handcuffed to a padlocked chain around a large fir, while Pagans mulled over their options as to reclaiming the house. Basically, there were two, Blue thought: Enter the house and force a surrender/shootout. Or, call for surrender and be prepared to lay siege until they give up. The latter was inherently safer, but ran the risk that the invaders might decide to set the house on fire and go out in a literal blaze of glory, especially if they saw themselves in a no-win situation. *Desperate people commit desperate acts.*

* * * * *

Amanita was the senior member of one of the secreted bivouacs. With her were Tad and Meadow. Gaia, the resident authority at the other camp, oversaw Owl, scared and uncomfortable out of his element, the slightly wounded, very uncomfortable Flora, and Diana, who saw this as an exciting adventure that she was mostly missing out on. Each camp was located off some intentionally obscure trails between a quarter and a half mile from the house and nearly that amount from each other. Coyote floated between the two camps pausing often, listening intently for invaders, prepared to give up his life in his comrades' defense. The camps' purpose was to hide away most of their weapons/tools/ food stocks/clothes, virtually all the portable valuables, in order to deny any support to invaders. But the camps were adequate sleep-over facilities as well, especially in mid-summer dry weather.

They had understood before hand there was to be no fire and no lights. Anyone who approached either bivouac unannounced was likely to get shot. Coyote and the other Pagans, knew to repeat, *Meet the new boss...* until they heard the response, *Same as the old boss.*

With nightfall fast approaching Amanita broke out meal rations and made sure Meadow and Tad had their bedrolls laid out in a concealed depression of the brushy terrain. As the only male in the group, Tad was trying to maintain a confident *persona*, but Amanita could see through it, could see the nervousness/anxiety here and there close to the surface. At nine, he was given the option of bearing a weapon or not; the argument being, unarmed, he had a credible, legitimate claim to being a child non-combatant, a civilian. He went for the weapons training without hesitation. He had a Walther .38 and was weighing the degree of security he felt with this lethal weapon.

Ok, so tell me the game plan one more time, if we get bandits coming up on us, Tad ventured, a little too nonchalantly.

Wishing she had more convincing details to add, regretting having to repeat the simple strategy, Amanita said, *Well, we'll have the element of surprise so we'll be able to pick them off before they shoot us. First of all, it is very unlikely the bad guys could make it this far from home base. But if this long-shot event takes place, I expect we'll hear 'em coming and shoot the shit out of 'em. Meadow and I've got the long guns, so we'll do the front line, distance shooting. You are our fallback defense, our close-range fighting.*

Though Amanita believed a direct breach of their position to be less likely an event than Tad, she remained uneasy, not just for herself or her unborn baby, but what this threat meant to the other tribal members, and their collective way of life.

From the earliest opportunity, Meadow was eager for the chance to shoot a lot of different guns. She was big for her age and got to be reasonably accurate with a .223 semi-automatic. Having worked the action of her rifle again, she loaded it with a clip of 10 cartridges and laid it beside her bedroll, then lay down next to it; she got the draw of snooze time for the next couple of hours. Tad could stay up, or sleep, as he liked, but with no Meadow to bounce off of, he was drifting into a nod of his own.

As their sole sentinel this late-evening hour, Amanita was indulging doubts of the wisdom of this strategy, hauling most of the house's portable valuables to be squirreled away in these hidden caches. At great human effort. The alternative, as she understood it, would've entailed defending the house with everything they had. She believed they would've been able to withstand assaults on the house with sand-bagged windows and better defenses. Most of the rest of the council didn't think the house was that defensible with, say, all the outbuildings in flames; their views had prevailed.

Spontaneously, with time, such unexpressed and unchallenged doubts have a way of spinning off into other realms: one's overall contentment index, for instance; one's confidence level might suffer. All this mayhem on top of her impending motherhood, which, she'd had abundant opportunity to consider, was not well timed. Without any inducement at all, she had about talked herself into a full-blown *pre*-partum anxiety episode when she heard the crackling of gunfire in the direction of the house, like the sound of firecrackers a couple of city streets over, a little muffled. Only, it was a lot of firecrackers going off all at once. Then just as suddenly, silence. Meadow and Tad continued sleeping, uninterrupted.

She didn't know what to make of so much shooting but she was pretty sure more people were dying. And both sides were shooting. She'd explored most of the plausible consequences of the firefight—having taken place as much as a half hour previously—when she heard another solitary shot, and nothing else. In some inexplicable way, this final shot—a coup de grace?—restored some hope. Or so she was feeling when she was shocked into realizing a person, or persons, was approaching. Grunting something. Cocking her rifle, Amanita leaned forward into the direction she'd heard the sounds concentrating all her visual and aural faculties: someone muttering... *newb osss.* Pause. *Eat th' new boss.* Pause.

It was Sparrow, risking getting shot, bringing news.

* * * * *

215

Considering their predicament over thermoses of hot tea and hard biscuits, Blue finally spoke, *Here's what I think: I doubt if they're going to voluntarily leave the house tonight, but I sure as hell don't want to stay out here all night making sure they don't try to fool us and run for it. And they just might get crazy-desperate enough to torch the place. We've got two good flashlights, right? I propose we sneak up there, and if we don't draw fire, enter our house and demand their surrender. In fact, those folks who want to stay back and secure the possible escape routes, that's fine by me,* allowing a delicate out for anyone not sanguine about walking into a blazing-guns scenario.

All five wanted to go along. Nobody argued for waiting; nobody wanted to miss the action. *Actually, the more I think of it, the more I see it's a good idea for a couple of us to stay back; six of us might be a bit much for a two-flashlight shootout. We'd be running a higher risk of shooting each other. Like Robbie said, there could be three of 'em, but realistically there's probably only two.* By scissors/rock/ paper, a visibly disappointed Yumi and Martel were chosen to stay back and cut off any exits.

Crow and Sparrow were stealthy in their approach to the house and entered the back door soundlessly. Blue and Waymer encountered a locked front door and nervously jiggled it, making too much noise in the process. Crow whispered to Sparrow to stay put near the back door while he quickly crossed the open space by feel and unbolted the lock. Once inside, they carefully searched the basement and the rooms on the first floor by flashlight: two dead bodies downstairs, one of them a young woman, Chance's body in one back bedroom and in the other, the guy shot in the lower spine, beyond unhappy. Delirious.

Some motion occurred upstairs, audibly indicating the location of the remaining holdouts. In his newly acquired command voice, Blue boomed, *Ok, guests, it's time to cut your best deal. Surrender now and we'll make it easier on you.* Complete silence. *Your comrades are all dead; you can't get away. If you make this hard for us, I promise it'll be hard on you, too.*

Still no sound from the second floor. Crow motions that he is going up, the others close behind. Inevitably the third step creaks when weight is put on it, and suddenly there is the loud crack of a pistol. Everyone winces and freezes in place. After a heart-racing minute, Crow resumes his assent and, again, the third step groans.

This time, a voice comes from above, *Don't shoot. I surrender.*

A long pause before Blue spoke. *Ok, show your hands and come downstairs.*

217

Four guns and two flashlight beams trained on the shaking, empty-handed man nearly stumbling down the stairs. He was quickly handcuffed while Crow and Waymer went up to verify the deathly silence upstairs. They encountered two more dead, one having just blown the back of his head off, barrel of the gun still in his mouth, body still warm, blood and brain matter still oozing out of the exit wound.

After securing the house, they returned their attention to their captive, who said, a trifle faux cheerfully, *Hey, Crow, Blue. It's me, Lenny.* Nodding in her direction, he said, *Sparrow, long time no see.*

Well I'll be go to hell, it is Lenny, exclaimed Blue. *The plot sickens! But first, a couple of flashlight folks should check the dorms and other buildings—no surprises, please. Then, hit the woods to give the all-clear. Another couple could get a fire going and see about some hot water; after, we'll chat with ol' Lenny, here, till the cows come home.*

I'll make the rounds, said Sparrow, abruptly, and was out the door.

Yeah, me too, Crow added. Martel and Yumi began collecting kindling and larger firewood for the stove.

It was the middle of the night but except for dead bodies stacked here and there, the place was functional, and Waymer and Blue settled in for a chat with their prisoner. *What a coincidence finding you here with these guys,* Blue said.

Yeah, I know what you mean, Lenny said. *I didn't have a choice; they woulda killed me if I didn't throw in with 'em.*

How long you been with 'em?

I don't know, maybe three months.

Whose idea was it to pay us a visit? Waymer asked.

Chigger's been working this riff for months now. He sweeps an area and he gets the locals to tell 'im who lives up the road.

In the manner applied by Attila, and Genghis Khan —the means by which the locals tell him...Blue muttered.

So who told him about us? Where we live?

They heard about you since Three Farms, trying hard to distance himself from his comrades with the third person plural pronoun; *they check out all the country roads for set-ups like this. I didn't lead 'em here, if that's what you think.*

Which one's Chigger? asked Waymer.

He's the one upstairs popped himself rather than let you guys catch 'im.

What were you going to do to us if you'd overrun us? asked Waymer.

I had some pull; I woulda asked for leniency. They woulda gone easy on you. Since I knew you, and all...

An involuntary shudder between the two Pagans while they considered the veracity of this last statement. *Who's the girl?* Blue asked.

Just a captured bitch who figured she had a better chance plundering along side them than being plundered. Which she was anyway, if you know what I mean.

Looks like she figured wrong, said Waymer.

Yeah, maybe. Not what you'd call an easy choice, either way.

The out buildings had been left pretty much intact; the invaders realized early on they'd better stick together in defense of the main house. Within the hour Sparrow and Crow had returned; however, she cut their prisoner a wide berth. Everyone was jubilant they'd retaken their homestead. Most would stay camped overnight where they were already settled in, and return home in the light of day.

A couple of Pagans helped Robbie hobble to the woodshed where he was given water and a blanket, and locked up. Nothing else was critical that night, nothing else needed deciding or adjudicating. Lenny was manacled to a freestanding beam and given a blanket. Waymer and Blue nodded out in the overstuffed chairs while the others went to the dorms to salvage what was left of the night.

Shortly after first light, Martel and Crow reinstalled the unplugged gravity-feed water system. Soon water was heating on the stove and people were starting the unsavory task of searching the bodies for weapons, identification and anything else of value, and stripping them of recyclable clothes. During the ordeal of stacking them in preparation for mass burial, Blue exclaimed, *Well, lookee here! This one's Rocco, one of the guys we fended off at Switzerland on our way to the powwow with the Stones. I wouldn't be surprised if ol' Toad is here somewhere.* Rocco had shot the kid goat and was, himself, shot and died over the course of the night in that no-man's land of a clearing between the backside of the house and the tree line.

Little by little the Pagans returned to the homestead. Their first inclination, after a reflexive glance at the invader dead, was to gawk at the two captives; the battlefield bleed out and the lower-spinal-cord-shot assailant died during the night. Sure enough, Flora discovered the bloodied remains of Rocco's partner, Toad, among the pile that had stormed out of the cabin in hopes of rescuing their vehicles —and into the trap that had cost their lives.

They got what was coming to 'em, I say, pronounced Crow. The sense of loss of Chance and Tooloose was universal, and tied Pagans together in their shared grief, their shared resolve to move beyond this

221

tragedy. Now, though, there was far too much to do to give public-shared vent to their sorrow.

Taybo was encouraged to have a close look at the two remaining invaders; Waymer accompanied him, a fly on the wall, to witness his reaction. Before Robbie, he spent several minutes silently watching, not revealing any emotion. But in merely approaching the seated Lenny, Taybo grew agitated. He stayed less than a minute and at that, off to one side, holding a hand over his mouth as if stifling a scream. He was clearly uncomfortable to be in this man's presence.

Waymer and Blue were eager to hear his account. He said he didn't have a specific memory of Robbie, so he stayed awhile to see if he could pick up some vibe, a nuanced feeling. In the end, he couldn't come up with a sense of Robbie, one way or the other. Either he hadn't seen him or he'd failed to make an impression.

With Lenny, however, it was quite different. He remembered Lenny all too well; Lenny enjoyed inflicting pain on Three-Farms folks. The people he singled out were chosen seemingly at random, and he took pleasure in watching their total abasement in trying to avoid more pain. Without warning and certainly without provocation, this man had jabbed him in the crotch with a stout, five-foot walking pole.

Waymer, Blue and Gaia convened an emergency session of elders to outline recovery issues and determine what to do with Robbie and Lenny. From what they'd learned talking to Robbie, he was a reluctant kill-or-be-killed participant; with him they remained ambivalent. Except that saving him almost surely meant amputating his leg below his shattered thigh bone, a serious undertaking, especially for Gaia. The first act of this incarnation of Pagan Elders was to agree to give Robbie the choice to convert wholly to the Pagans, and submit to all the rules—and endure having his leg cut off—or his "freedom," meaning abandonment. Someone posited the argument that it was hardly a fair choice. Waymer's response: *What's fair? He* _did_ *ride into our lives with a gang bent on subjugating and/or killing us all. Fuck fair!*

In announcing his choice, Robbie sounded thoroughly convincing—knowing his life depended on it!— in his desire to commit the rest of his life to the success of the Haven. It remained to be seen how well that would play out. Gaia and Blue, with a cast of helpers, agreed to take on —sorry, take *off*—the, by now, gangrenous and increasingly putrid leg the following morning.

The fate of Lenny, however, was more problematic. Gaia wondered what Sparrow's avoidance of Lenny might mean, remembering that she first came to them with

Lenny. Blue thought she was nearby on a cleaning project and volunteered to fetch her.

We're trying to get our bearings in a post-Chance tribe, said Waymer, as soon as she arrived. *One of the most pressing matters is what to do about our captives. We were wondering if you had any thoughts-slash-feelings about Lenny...*

I was afraid you'd ask me that, Sparrow confessed, *but glad to get it out in the open. We'd been together for some time when we came here and split up. I do have some positive feelings about the guy, in the form of memories. On the other hand, I'm so pissed at him, so betrayed by his part in attacking us, that I don't care what happens to him.*

Be careful what you say, Blue said. *We've heard a disturbing report about him—via Taybo—and we're considering his involvement in all this a capital offense.*

A fifteen-second pause that felt like two minutes. In a measured, unambiguous voice, she said, *I would be in complete accordance with a capital-offence verdict on Lenny.*

The two men were mum to Lenny regarding the meeting of the elders and Taybo's account. *Here's some tea and a biscuit. After that, you're gonna have to help us prepare a burial site,* Blue said.

You're shittin me, right? Because that's, like, slave labor, which is prohibited by the Geneva Conventions.

Oh, Waymer groaned in mock-anguished tones, *I shoulda 'membered 'bout dem nasty ol' Geneva Conventions,* slapping his forehead with the palm of his hand, in character. Spinning it out in slipstream vernacular, *If the cities around here don't survive in any meaningful sense, what hope is there for Geneva? I'd like to think there's still a Geneva; beautiful city!* still on a roll. Then, in Lenny's face, in full menace, *So shut the fuck up. If you don't shut it, you're gonna be sucking on your split lip instead of a nice cup of tea and a biscuit,* indicating with the butt of his rifle how the split lip, and possibly a broken-out tooth or two, might be accomplished in the blink of an eye.

Blue this time: *So have the tea and biscuit or don't, but in about 10 minutes, you are going to help us dig a hole. Or you are going to get acquainted with prolonged, significant pain, only this time from the position of the recipient, and not the dispenser of suffering, the role you liked so much. It'll be our version of the sort you used to dole out to helpless people,* leaving him to ponder which in particular they had in mind.

Over the next couple of hours, truculent, sulking the whole time, Lenny dug the equivalent of half the pit, his

225

digging partners traded off on the other half, always under the watchful eye of someone with the 12-gauge shotgun at the ready. During this time, a rotating crew brought out the bodies by stretcher and wheelbarrow. When the pit had reached at least five feet deep, six wide by ten feet long, Crow, the last one to dig with Lenny, got boosted out.

Lenny was told to hold his hands up so that his cuffs could be removed. When he tried to climb out, he got the back of a shovel hard across his face. He slumped back into the hole, trying to ride out the blinding, pulsing pain radiating from his smashed nose. Seated with his back to an earthen wall, he was beginning to staunch the blood on his shirtsleeve, when the bodies started falling on him. At first, with great effort he was able to wriggle out from under them; eventually they pinned his legs and his torso, him pleading, *Lemme outa here!* in a diminishing voice. Twenty dead people account for a significant mass of bodies.

Make that twenty-one.

* * * * *

The matter was never formally spoken of. It is not known who wielded the fateful shovel. Some people were participants and thereby knew all there was to know, others knew as much as they wanted. Still others had not participated or been privy to the information; most considered themselves fortunate to be out of this particular information loop.

Sparrow was not known to have ever inquired. Sometimes, ignorance really is bliss. Let fading demons be gone! No one questioned the decision, at the time or after. Except that evening at their modest dinner, when Tad asked what had become of all the dead people.

We buried all those who attacked us but Robbie up the slope there, Coho said, gesturing the direction with his fork.

What about Lenny? continued Tad, Meadow and Diana all ears.

Simultaneously, Waymer and Gaia made the universal gesture for silence: a vertical pointer finger up against pursed lips. Later, in private, Waymer told Tad they were mourning Chance and Tooloose, and it was inappropriate to talk about those people who had attacked them. A bit of a cop out, to be sure. After, though, he was less apt to ask.

Everyone felt the loss of Chance and Tooloose in his/her own, usually private way, but Meadow appeared genuinely traumatized by the loss. Soon thereafter, as if mentored by Meadow, Tad, and to a lesser extent, Diana succumbed to their older sister's melancholia. If Chance had seemed a father figure, Tooloose was their look-up-to, straight-up, main-man role model. For the younguns, with Owl the exception, it was a double-sided funk. The Owl-man internalized his reactions, Mr. Practical appeared not to struggle with grief. Maybe later. At council that first evening, everyone acknowledged the issue and vowed to include the youths in as many activities as possible—in lieu of ideas of what else they might be doing.

Meanwhile, far more immediately compelling matters demanded their attention. This simply wasn't the time to wallow in sorrow, or anger, or grief, not to speak of fear. The Pagans had to bury two of their own, quickly revive their suspended agriculture efforts, and perform an amputation, an event not even Gaia had ever experienced. Also, they had a birth to prepare for, perhaps no more than two weeks away. At a psychic level, they faced the absolute necessity of adapting to the changed makeup of the household, and the need to reinforce and nurture the tribal identity at every step.

Preliminary assessment had it that the vegetable garden had been trampled, but was mostly salvageable; little was set back from most of the week's neglect—four days on high alert, the battle day and today, a day of recovery and assessment. The soybean patch was coming along nicely—*tofu* by next winter!—and their experimental

Ethiopian grain, *teff*, was doing better than anyone imagined possible. Also, the patches of wheat, oats, and barley had seen little damage.

Harvest was going to present its own set of complications. Hopefully, the harvest time for each crop would stagger. This was everyone's first grain harvest coming up; they didn't know what to expect. Everything would be done by hand, inventing devices and techniques to streamline the process as they went along. It was humbling to admit that, in knowledge of agricultural techniques and procedures, they were a good deal more ignorant than the average person of their grandparents' generation, and were starting out being little better than farmers from the Middle Ages.

A future holiday—maybe Thanksgiving, they still had much to be thankful for, after all—might be a good time to lick their wounds, give voice to their feelings about what they had endured, and how they were managing to carry on. For now, however, the race was on to lay in enough stores to make it through the implacably approaching winter.

* * * * *

...Flight of the sea birds,
scattered like lost words,
wheel to the storm in flight...
Fare thee well now,
let your life proceed by its own design.
Nothing to tell now;
let the words be yours,
I am done with mine.

> *Cassidy,*
> The Grateful Dead

American post mortem

In hindsight, it is hard to fathom how we could not have seen this coming, except to say we didn't *want* to see it coming. What kind of wretched contrarian would go against the grain—no, that's too jagged and splintery a metaphor— what fool would try to swim up river when everything and everyone else went with the flow, floating tranquilly, gently down the stream: *Merrily, merrily, merrily, merrily life is but a dream.* Who would want to give up that incredibly indulgent "dream"? If you were born into opulence, and certainly this included the average American relative to three-quarters of the rest of the world, it is not too difficult to see how a lifestyle of hyper-consumption might be seen as one's entitlement. A birthright, if you will. Each adult with his/her own vehicle. Three or four televisions per household. A cell phone for every family member: America, the only society to elevate not mere materialism, but utter, wallow-in-it profligacy, to the level of an enviable lifestyle, a virtue.

But surely we deserved these gifts by being God-fearing, freedom-loving citizens, a veritable beacon to the world. Do every nation's citizens believe their government's propaganda? No matter, certainly we Americans did. In the end, America had become a paper tiger, a pretend-wizard behind the hanging bedsheet, a hollowed-out shell of our former eminence intimidating the world for a time with our chutzpah and panegyrics, gulling her citizens in the process. Still coasting 40 years later from the post-WWII political, cultural, military, and economic high-water mark, frantically clutching at the hollow imagery of those years. The mythos of a once-great nation reduced to platitude, mawkish bluster, and "smart bombs."

Our cultural exports, a mix of styles in music and the performing arts, had for decades captivated far-flung nations and were aped in curious corners of the world. Whole industries promoted little more than *style*—a posture or attitude to the world: What it was like to be cool —to dazzle, intrigue, hypnotize, to ooze *joie de vivre,* to further seduce an already benumbed public. Meanwhile content, to be delicate, had been wanting for some time; what had constituted the substance of the economy for the first two centuries of her existence, manufacturing, in terms of the US GDP, was increasingly anemic. Complacent, oblivious, or stuporous, Americans dimly perceived offshore innovation and production displacing ours. Except for international banking, and the munitions/weapons industries, of course. In these fields alone, for too long we were unequaled in all the world, leading the parade into the abyss: *Join us in fighting terrorists in far-off lands! Buy our indebtedness; buy our funny-paper promissory notes!*

With these twin hammers, this double whammy of overwhelmingly dominant military capability—in settings of traditional warfare—and waning-but-still-controlling financial clout via the World Bank, Wall Street, and US leverage with the IMF, most other countries were harried into doing our bidding. So they silently bore it, resenting it for decades, biding their time. *Pax Americana* had become *Pox Americana,* the American affliction, hastening the downfall of civilization. When a flank was finally exposed (the economy, at last?), and the more intrepid among the jackals began tearing at the still-twitching flesh— *disembowelment on Prime Time TV!*—a kind of spontaneous, widespread *schadenfreude* emerged; the satisfaction one feels in seeing Mista Big toppled, the giddy pleasure in bringing down Numba One. Behold, the mighty brought to its knees!

We weren't paying attention when enough was enough, so it became too much. Too much is and always will be too much—in a word, unsustainable. Such was the volatile state of *realpolitik* at the cusp of the second decade of the 21st C.

Bibliography

My desire, in presenting this list, is to give the reader a sense of the published works that nudged and prodded me to tell this story.

Non-fiction:

Bacevich, A. J. (2008). *The Limits of Power, The End of American Exceptionalism*. NY: Metropolitan Books.

Berman, M. (2000). *The Twilight of American Culture*. NY: W. W. Norton.

Bourdieu, P. (1998). *Practical Reason*. (Trans, by G. Sapiro, R. Johnson, and L. Wacquant). Stanford, CA: Stanford University Press.

Brown, L. R. (2001). *Eco-economy: Building an Economy for the Earth*. NY: W. W. Norton.

Chomsky, N. (2002). *9-11*. NY: Seven Stories Press.

Dawkins, R. (2006). *The God Delusion*. NY: Houghton Mifflin.

Diamond, J. (2005). *Collapse, How Societies Choose to Fail or Succeed*. NY: Penguin Books.

Diamond, J. (1999). *Guns, Germs, and Steel, The Fates of Human Societies*. NY: W. W. Norton.

Diamond, J. (1992). *The Third Chimpanzee, The Evolution and Future of the Human Animal*. NY: HarperCollins.

Frank, T. (2004). *What's the Matter with Kansas? How the Conservatives Won the Heart of America*. NY: Henry Holt and Co.

Goodman, A. and Goodman, D. (2006). *Static: Government Liars, Media Cheerleaders, and the People Who Fight Back*. NY: Hyperion.

Hedges, C. (2006). *American Fascists: The Christian Right and the War on America*. NY: Free Press.

Korten, D. C. (2009). *Agenda for a New Economy, From Phantom Wealth to Real Wealth*. San Francisco, CA: Berrett-Koehler.

Korten, D. C. (2006). *The Great Turning: From Empire to Earth Community*. San Francisco, CA: Berrett-Koehler.

Kunstler, J. H. (2005). *The Long Emergency: Surviving the Long Catastrophes of the Twenty-first Century*. NY: Atlantic Monthly Press.

Layton, P. (2002). *Emergency Food Storage & Survival Handbook: Everything You Need to Know to Keep Your Family Safe in a Crisis*. NY: Three Rivers Press.

Lundberg, J. (2005). End-time for USA upon oil collapse. Culture Change Letter #100. http://www.culturechange.org/e-letter-archive.html

Orr, D. W. (2004). *The Last Refuge, Patriotism, Politics, and the Environment in an Age of Terror*. Washington DC: Island Press.

Murphy, C. (2007). *Are We Rome? The Fall of an Empire and the Fate of America*. NY: Houghton Mifflin.

Perkins, J. (2004). *Confessions of an Economic Hit Man*. San Francisco, CA: Berrett-Koehler.

Pollan, M. (2002). *The Botany of Desire: A Plant's-eye View of the World*. NY: Random House.

Pollan, M. (2006). *The Omnivore's Dilemma: A Natural History of Four Meals*. NY: Penguin Press.

Prugh, T., Costanza, R., Daly, H. (2000). *The Local Politics of Global Sustainability*. Washington DC: Island Press.

Roberts, P. (2004). *The End of Oil, On the Edge of a Perilous New World*. NY: Houghten Mifflin.

Weisman, A. (1998). *Gaviotas: A village to reinvent the world*. White River Jct, VT: Chelsea Green.

Weisman, A. (2007). *The World Without Us*. NY: St. Martin's Press.

www.culturechange.org

www.hubbertpeak.com

www.lifeaftertheoilcrash.net

www.peakoil.com

www.postcarbon.org

Zinn, H. (2001). *A People's History of the United States, 1492-Present*. NY: Perennial Classics.

Speculative fiction:

Kunstler, J. H. (2008). *World Made by Hand*. NY: Atlantic Monthly Press.

McCarthy, C. (2006). *The Road*. NY: Vintage Books.

Rawls, J. W. (2006). *Patriots: Surviving the Coming Collapse: A Novel of the Near Future*. No location cited: Clearwater Press.

Acknowledgements

Many people contributed to this story, but it got its real poke in the ribs from the various malingerers at periodic Small River pilgrimages: Tumor, Jambles, Grunt, Quarrel, Red Dog, and my brother, Phip. All offered substantial feedback, often in the form of sniggers, guffaws, rolled eyes, hoots, raspberries, retching sounds and other such sly signals, that my simple narrative was making a strong impression.

In addition, I want to acknowledge my editor and old high school friend, James Livingston, for his careful guidance and encouragement. Grant Nelson, also, offered much constructive advice. And Burt Jurgens has been an immense help in guiding me through the labyrinth of the publishing process. Finally, a deep bow of gratitude to my wife, Mikiko, for enduring an obsessive/compulsive, muttering recluse of a husband for too much of the previous two years.

On a different note I wish to acknowledge what many astute readers will have noted already. I knowingly flaunted a spelling convention six or eight times in the text

—may the wrath of the Spelling Police smite me! English "permits" *somehow, somewhere, somewhat, something,* and *someone*. But not *somesuch!?* Try it; type it into your MS Word document. That wavy red line under your proposed spelling tells you it is incorrect, not to be countenanced, ba-a-aaad.

What's the rationale, here? It is my position that we can know the conventional spelling and still exhibit an element of non-compliance in the face of arbitrary, counterintuitive rules. Or somesuch.

Tuna Cole
Portland, OR
July 2009

For more information, please visit
www.ragnarokaplausiblefuture.com